FIREWATCH.

By Cynthia Wall, KA7ITT

Published by the
American Radio Relay League
Newington, CT USA 06111

D1167159

Cover and illustrations by Sheila Dianne Somerville

For my brother,
Steve Jensen
W6RHM

CONTENTS

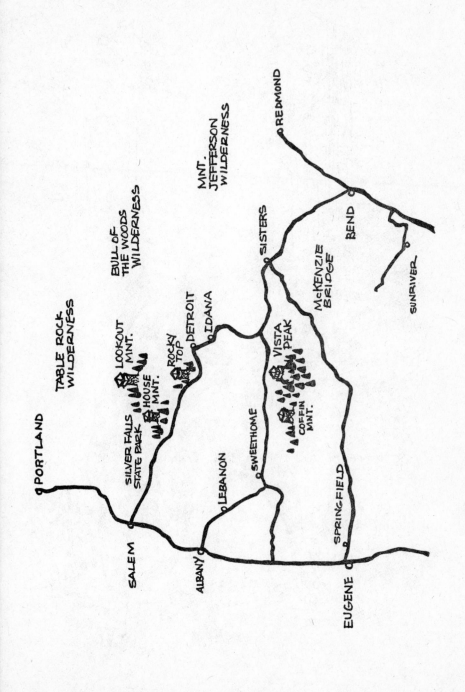

Chapter 1

Hunger!

Friday, June 10th, 8 a.m.
Oregon Cascades
3 Miles SW of Vista Peak Lookout

Brutus was hungry. Hungry with an intensity that shook his sixty-pound muscular body. He raised his head, sniffed the wind, and turned his cold almond-shaped eyes vacantly toward the edge of the grove of tall firs. That was the direction the man always came—the tall man who smelled of tobacco and sweat and dried leaves. When the man came, he rarely spoke, but he carried a large pan of kibble and sometimes a raw bone for Brutus to gnaw.

Brutus's taut brindle-colored body trembled with the memory of food. Saliva dripped from his massive v-shaped jaws that were twice as strong as those of a German Shepherd. Jaws that could kill or maim with a single bone-crunching bite. The hunger that had begun as a flicker three days ago when the man left had now grown to a raging fire.

If Brutus had been anything other than a Pit Bull, he might have howled or barked his complaints to the wind. But the squat, heavily muscled dogs were bred to be silent. Some of them were also bred and trained to be killers. Not all of them. Raised with love and care, they could be loyal pets. But when teased and baited and trained to kill, they learned to do their masters' bidding with savage quickness.

In Brutus's litter, one pup had gone to a family with children to be raised as a faithful and gentle friend. Two others were sold to men who claimed they wanted the dogs as guards—in reality, they wanted to cultivate the fierce genes lying dormant in the dogs. Then the dogs would be used in

1

illegal fights where men would bet money on which dog could kill the other.

Brutus's background was somewhere in between. For a short while, he had lived with a family with a ten-year old girl. A girl who petted him and rubbed his small ears and patted his sleek body. She said nice things to him, and she smelled like flowers and fresh air. Her pockets always held treats for him. The memory of that happy time was tucked somewhere in his brain cells behind the hunger message.

All of that had been before the girl's parents started quarreling. The shouts had gone on and on and the girl cried a lot. Brutus licked the salty tears from her face. Then the father in the house had left and Brutus was sold. A tall, quiet man came and took him away in a truck—kept him in a garage where he kicked him and taunted him with sticks.

When Brutus began to attack any object that was held out to him, the man grunted with satisfaction. Then he took him in the truck to this place deep in the forest that smelled so strange. Here he was chained night and day to a sturdy dog-house—chained with heavy metal links that even Brutus's powerful jaws couldn't break. Until this week, the man had come back usually every day—sometimes with another man—bringing food.

Now the hunger grew and Brutus's stomach rumbled. He stood and rippled the muscles of his body, nose to tail. He turned around and around and lay down in the dried fir needles. Then he stood again. In his brain, hunger and hatred melted into one—his instinct as a killer fired the urges, and he tossed his head restlessly back and forth. He lifted his nose.

There was a new scent on the wind—one that triggered the old memories of the girl. A sweet scent like flowers. It was mingled with another smell—the pungent odor of sweating horses and mules. The sound of a dog barking in the distance made his ears prick forward with even greater attention. He drew air into his powerful lungs and tasted it as it floated past his nose and throat. For a brief moment, he had that pleasant feeling that he had when he lived at the girl's house—the feeling of being warm and cared for. But then the hunger drove it away. The scent of the girl merged with the fire in his brain, and he quivered violently. Brutus was ready to kill.

Chapter 2

A Home in the Sky

Friday, June 10th, 8 a.m.
On the trail to Vista Peak Lookout*

"KA7SJP from W7QMU." Kim jumped slightly at the man's voice coming from the Amateur Radio transceiver attached to her belt. The sturdy brown trail horse flicked his ears questioningly at the voice. Kim switched the reins to her right hand and reached down to pat him reassuringly before answering the call.

"W7QMU this is KA7SJP—name's Kim and I'm with a mule train on my way up to Vista Peak Lookout—just heard your call. Where are you?"

To Kim's utter amazement, Jack, the leader of the pack train turned around in his saddle and waved. His hand held a transceiver similar to Kim's.

"Jack? You're a ham? Why didn't you tell me? I had no idea."

Jack chortled into his microphone, and Kim imagined his whiskered face smiling in merriment.

"I was getting such a kick listening to you tell us all about what a perfect location this was going to be for DX (far away stations) and how excited you were. Part of me wanted to agree with you and tell you about my experiences years ago working a crystal set in this very lookout. But a bigger part of me wanted to be quiet and just surprise you."

"Well you certainly did that," Kim laughed. "How long have you been an Amateur Radio operator?"

"Thirty-five years exactly," Jack said. "Got my license the same year I joined the Forest Service. And it's the best thing I ever did."

*Vista Peak is a fictitious name.

4

"I guess that explains why you didn't complain when I asked if there would be room on the mules to bring my radio gear."

"Yup," said Jack happily. "In fact, I've got some extra wire here in the saddlebags to help you string an antenna."

"I can't believe this," Kim laughed into her mike. "Fortune is certainly smiling on me today."

Jack waved again to her and then turned his attention to guiding his bay mare, "Cleo," over a rocky part of the trail.

Kim smiled with anticipation. A friend of hers had told her in April about the summer openings with the Forest Service for fire lookouts. The friend, Ann, had declared that she would go crazy all cooped up in a glass box on top of a mountain. But the minute Kim heard about the job, she knew she wanted it.

Now here she was on her way to the Vista Peak Lookout. Her sleeping bag, three changes of clothes, astronomy books, knitting, writing tablets, and am-fm radio were all strapped on the mule ahead of her. The saddlebags of the horse she rode bulged with her TS-440 transceiver and power supply—radio gear she hoped would allow her to talk to the entire world from her mountaintop perch.

Kim was so fond of her "rig" that she had affectionately nicknamed it "Jessie." Her family and her boyfriend, Marc, often teased her about Jessie's exploits: talking to the Space Shuttle, relaying emergency traffic from earthquake victims in Mexico, or just providing the enjoyable communication link between Kim and other Amateur Radio operators around the world.

The last mule of the train carried food and water. Kim had been told by the U.S. Forest Service that she would be visited by mule train every thirty days so that she would have to gauge her supplies—especially water—carefully, and not be wasteful of anything.

Now as they neared the mountaintop, Kim gasped in wonder at the view. The valleys of the Oregon Cascades were spread below outlined by heavy stands of fir, hemlock, and alder. Normally, the valleys and mountains were rich green this early in June, but an unusually dry spring had already started to brown the vista.

"This may be a busy summer for you, Kim," Joe Beardsley, the forestry official in charge of the lookouts had told her. She had listened carefully to all of his instructions and to stories told her by experienced lookouts. An intensive training session had taught her how to use the fire-finding equipment, and she had quickly memorized the protocol for reporting smoke or fire.

The burden of being responsible for the safety of the forests made her a little nervous, but on this bright, early summer day, Kim felt up to just about anything. She whistled softly to "Bart," Jack's Australian Shepherd who accompanied him just about everywhere. The black and gray dog came running from the underbrush he had been investigating.

"Bart's one of the benefits of being semi-retired," Jack had told her laughingly. "I set my own hours, I take my dog with me, and I spend as much time on the ham radio as I want to."

Bart trotted back from the mule train and panted happily up at Kim. Tendrils of wild flowers clung to his silver-black fur, and his nose was dirty from exploring small animal burrows. He barked in greeting to Kim.

"Wish I could keep you up here with me," Kim said to the dog. Even though it would certainly ease loneliness, she had decided against having a pet in the lookout. Coyotes ranged the mountains and there were too many risks for a domestic pet.

Well, she'd just count on her Amateur Radio to keep her company. Being totally alone would be a new experience for her, and Kim faced it with a mixture of anticipation and slight worry.

"I've got lots to do," she said to the dog who had decided to trot alongside her mule for awhile. He wagged his tail at her words so she kept on talking. "First project is to lose the ten pounds I gained on dormitory food this year in college." She patted her tummy and again the dog wagged his tail and barked in agreement.

"That's not polite," she teased the dog. "You're supposed to say, 'No, Kim, you look just fine to me.'"

The dog barked again.

"That's better," laughed Kim.

Food had been a big topic of discussion in her preparations for the mountaintop.

"Don't you want some canned meat or stew or something with some substance in it?" her mother had asked as Kim laid out her supplies on the kitchen table.

"Nope," Kim said firmly—"I'm going to try to live on beans and rice—less packaging, less waste, and less calories."

But in the end, her mother managed to tuck a few cans of tuna into the bulging knapsacks, along with some frozen spaghetti sauce and a sealed container of her homemade chocolate chip cookies. Kim had bought some carrots, potatoes, apples, and a few other fruits and vegetables that would keep well. She wasn't fond of coffee, but she included several kinds of tea to fix as a hot morning drink.

"There she is," came Jack's voice over Kim's radio.

Kim shaded her eyes with her hand against the morning sun and stared in the direction of Jack's pointing finger. A small glass cupola amidst the craggy summit rocks greeted them as they rounded the last corner of the dirt trail. Now the trail turned to loose shale and rock, and Kim and Jack quickly dismounted to lead the pack up the last hundred yards to the lookout.

Jack laughed as Kim hastily tied the reins of her horse and practically vaulted up the steps to the lookout. Like a bride inspecting her new home, she ran around the observation deck and peered excitedly through the windows.

"Here," said Jack pulling a key from his pocket. "Looks good—some years we have some trouble with vandalism, but I think this one came through okay."

"Oh!" Kim said standing in the middle of the 16 foot by 16 foot room. "Oh, it's just like a little house."

Jack grinned as he watched her poke the mattress on the high platform bed in one corner and run her hand along the top of the small propane refrigerator and stove. There were two small cupboards equipped with cooking utensils and a row of shelves underneath the windows for her books. She opened the door of the small woodstove and peeked inside.

Centered in the room was the Osborne Fire Finder, a large compass that would allow her to locate the heading in degrees of any smoke or fire. She had spent time at headquarters learning how to use it. Now Jack ran through the fire-reporting procedures again for her and showed her how to use the two-way radio that connected her to both the other lookouts and the Fire Dispatch Centers. A page of radio procedures was taped on the counter next to the radio.

"Now for the real radio," he said helping Kim to hook up "Jessie," her powerful transceiver that would link her to the world. For several hours, Kim and Jack worked together, first installing the solar panels that would charge her two 12 amp-hour gel cell batteries. Even with the sun charging them for 12 hours a day, she would have to run her transceiver at half power if she wanted to be able to talk for longer than an hour.

Kim chatted happily with Jack as she unpacked a whole bag of spare batteries for emergencies—batteries for the big rig, batteries for the two-way Forest Service radios that she would monitor constantly, and two battery packs for her small two-meter rig that she had used talking to Jack on the mule train. She even had a charge adapter for those packs that could plug into the power generated by the solar panels, but obviously she could charge them only during sunlight hours.

After the radio gear was installed to both of their satisfaction, and her two-meter antenna was attached to the side of the building, Kim unrolled the long 33-foot dipole antenna for "Jessie."

"Oooh," she said leaning over the balcony on the south side of the platform. The drop down the sheer rock wall seemed bottomless. "Guess I don't want to run the antenna down there."

"Here," said Jack. He handed her one end of the twenty-meter dipole antenna while he attached the other end to her outhouse north of the lookout.

"Perfect distance," Jack said, giving her the thumbs up signal.

"Glad that building will have more than one use," Kim said laughing.

She walked back inside and stowed her clothing in the drawers below the platform bed. After Jack left, she would arrange her books and other belongings, but already it was beginning to look like home. Kim felt a surge of satisfaction.

Jack was busy unloading her food supplies and piling them on the small counter. Kim put the food away quickly and then pulled two sandwiches from her backpack.

"Lunch?" she questioned Jack.

"Sure." He poured them each a glass of the precious water and they walked out to the warm sun on the catwalk surrounding the lookout. They sat in companionable silence, eating the sandwiches and gazing at the panoramic view. Jack handed her one of two pairs of high-power binoculars. She focused the lenses and then started studying the mountains and valleys below.

"You'll become as familiar with the landscape as the furniture in your own home," one of the lookouts had told her. Kim held a map in one hand and glanced at it tentatively. Mt. Jefferson, Iron Mountain—the names would become friends. And so would the other lookouts that she would be talking to by radio. Together, the forest lookouts would be the eyes that protected everything that lived and grew in their domain.

"I know what you're thinking," Jack said smiling. "Probably the same thoughts I had when I first came up here —quite a responsibility, huh?"

Kim nodded in agreement.

"Well you'll be surprised how quickly you'll get used to it. Just make sure you scan the area at least every fifteen minutes. Learn the topography as fast as you can, and soon you'll be an old pro."

"I just hope I do a good job," she said.

"I know you will," Jack said reassuringly.

He pointed out more of the landmarks for Kim, having her repeat the names of the major peaks until he was satisfied she had a general idea of the terrain.

Suddenly, Kim looked at her watch.

"Oh, I almost forgot—it's one, and I was going to try to call Marc on the Portland repeater. He's working for his uncle in construction this summer, but he said he'd listen for me at noon and one."

"Marc?" Jack questioned. "Boyfriend?"

"Yeah, friend, boyfriend," Kim said blushing a little. "Sometime when you've got about a week, I'll tell you about him. We've been through a lot together."*

"Well, I'd like to hear those stories," Jack said, but Kim was already calling Marc on the two-meter rig.

"KA7ITR from KA7SJP—are you there, Marc?"

"KA7SJP from KA7ITR—hi Kim, I hear you perfectly. Are you at the lookout yet?"

"Yes, I am and oh, Marc, it's beautiful. You can't believe how far I can see. And guess what? The packer who leads the mule trains up here is W7QMU..."

She chattered on happily, and Jack got up to let them talk alone. He loaded the empty saddlebags on the mules and made a final inspection of the lookout and Kim's setup.

She signed off with Marc and came over to the railing.

"You're not leaving, are you?"

"Yeah, time to be getting back pretty soon, but first I want to show you a little of your surroundings. Call the Ranger Station and tell them you'll be away from the post for about an hour."

Kim joined him as they hiked down the trail to a nearby stream. Jack showed her where the water dip was in case she ran out of water.

---

*You can read more about Kim and Marc's previous adventures in *Night Signals* (January 1990) and *Hostage in the Woods* (December 1990), both published by the American Radio Relay League.

"We used to have no qualms about drinking the stream water, but now if you have to use it, you should purify it. It's better not to drink it at all, and if you want to use it for bathing, carry the water well away from the edge. It's going to take a huge effort from humanity to keep our mountain waterways from getting any more polluted than they already are."

Kim giggled. She couldn't quite imagine stripping out here in the woods, but maybe, as Jack said, if she was brave enough and hot enough. They finished the brief tour and soon it was time for Jack to head back down the hill.

"Well, I'm only as far away as your two-meter rig," Jack said. "I monitor the local repeater every morning while I eat breakfast. And you know, if you have any kind of emergency, you just get on the forestry radio—there's always someone at headquarters and the other lookouts can answer questions for you too."

They talked for a few more minutes, and Kim shook his hand and patted the horses, mules, and Bart good-bye.

Jack glanced at his watch.

"Three o'clock. In three more hours, you'll be off duty. Best times are the evenings," Jack said smiling. "That's when I used to do my star gazing and my talking to the world. Quite a feeling to look up at the sky and know as the stars are shining down on you, the sun may be shining on the person you're talking to in Australia."

Kim grinned. She could hardly wait. She stood and watched Jack and the mule team until they disappeared around the corner of the trail. Then she grabbed the binoculars and did the first of her quarterly hour inspections of the area. With the map spread out before her, she glanced back and forth from the binoculars to the map, making mental notes of the names of each mountain peak.

At first she was so slow with her inspections that practically fifteen minutes elapsed before she completed her visual sweep and had to start again. But along about 5 o'clock, she started to feel confident. She was just putting down the binoculars and thinking she might have time to start a pot of rice for dinner when a small white wisp off to the southeast caught her attention. Quickly, she grabbed the binoculars and focused on the area. Gray and white smoke was pluming toward the sky. With her heart thudding, Kim grabbed the microphone to the forestry radio.

Chapter 3

Vista Peak Rookie

A split second before Kim depressed the transmit button on her forestry radio, she heard a low male voice boom over the radio.

"Dispatch Center, this is Lookout Mountain with a smoke report."

"Go ahead, Lookout Mountain."

Kim listened as he gave exact coordinates for the smoke.

"Azimuth 120 degrees, 30 minutes, Township 11 south, Range 6 east, Section 25, NE Corner. It's one and a half miles southeast of Buck Mountain, small white column."

After the dispatcher assigned an incident number to the report, Kim quickly called in a cross shot with her azimuth she had taken from the fire finder. The two smoke sightings would allow the dispatch center to determine the exact location. Shaking, she put down the microphone, feeling a mixture of relief and frustration. Relief that she had seen the fire in time to give a cross shot call but also frustration that she hadn't been the first to get the call in.

She had heard stories of how competitive the reporting could get. All lookouts liked to be the best, and being the first to call in a fire was definitely the way to prove you were on the job. However, working together for the benefit of the forests was more important than being first. With so few lookouts, all of them needed to work together cooperatively to provide the best fire protection.

Kim picked up her binoculars and scanned the area again. In a few minutes, she spotted forest service trucks moving along a road leading toward the fire. The smoke area wasn't getting any bigger, and pretty soon it started to diminish. She guessed it was somebody's campfire that hadn't been extin-

guished properly, and that now it was being mopped up by the fire workers.

At six o'clock, Kim heard the various lookouts calling in to go out of service for the night. She added her lookout to the list.

"Vista Peak out of service."

During the off duty hours of the lookouts, the mountains and valleys would be guarded by the "ALDS" (Automated Lightning Detection System), lightning detection devices located on mountaintops. But even with these aids, Kim had been told that a good lookout was always vigilant, and in the case of a fire threat, she could call Dispatch and put herself back in service. After all the check-ins at six o'clock, there was another call on the Forest Service radio. This time it was directed to her.

"Vista Peak from Coffin Mountain."

Kim jumped at the female voice calling her. Grabbing the microphone, she answered, "This is Vista Peak—go ahead Coffin Mountain."

"Hi, is this Kim? Welcome to the high country. My name's Alyse and we heard that you were an Amateur Radio operator too. Want to meet us on simplex so we don't tie up the radio?"

Eagerly, Kim agreed. She switched her two-meter radio to the simplex frequency and greeted her caller.

"This is KA7SJP on frequency."

The woman answered her immediately.

"Hi KA7SJP. This is N7NYJ, Alyse, and here's my husband, Frank, K6ELR. We're a husband and wife team up in the Coffin Mountain Lookout—been doing this for years. Heard this was your first time up and we wanted to welcome you."

Kim smiled at the warm friendliness in their voices. In the conversation that followed, she had a thousand questions for them. Who were the other lookouts? What was the secret for calling in the smokes first? What kind of Amateur Radio equipment did they have and did they work many stations?

"Whoa, Kim," Alyse came back to her. "One thing at a time."

Alyse told her a little about other lookouts in the area. She went on to tell her that the secret to calling a suspected fire in first was being topnotch on the fire finder so that you could locate coordinates quickly—also just being really observant when scanning.

"But just relax, Kim. It will get easier every day."

Then she went on to tell her of one lookout who had called in a fiery full moon as a fire on her first night in the tower.

Kim laughed. "Well, maybe I'm not the rookie of the year, but I sure do feel new at all this."

"And I bet you haven't eaten dinner yet, either?" Frank said.

"No," Kim admitted, "but I haven't had time to feel hungry."

"You eat dinner and if you have any problems, you give us a call on the Forest Service radio. We're not supposed to tie it up for chit chat, so if we want to talk for any length, we can move to two meters, and of course we need to watch our battery time on that. I hope you have a charger."

Kim told them she did and explained the solar equipment that Jack had helped her install. She listened intently as Frank described their setup. Since there were two of them, one of them could leave at any time. Alyse promised to drive over to the Vista Peak trailhead and hike up to visit Kim during the coming week.

Kim would have liked to talk to them for hours, but she didn't want to risk being left with dead batteries for the night. Reluctantly, she told them both goodnight and turned off the rig. She plugged the battery pack into the adapter connected to the gel cells even though she knew the solar unit had been in operation for only a few hours—probably not enough to store much power.

There was a second battery pack to use during the night, if needed. In the coming days, Kim planned to keep track of exactly how long her power would last with each rig to gauge her transmitting time appropriately. Maximum time on the air was a priority!

With a feeling of satisfaction, she looked around at the mountains surrounding the lush valleys below. Now Kim was part of the force protecting them and felt proud—give her a few weeks and she would become the guardian of the forests she wanted to be!

Time to fix dinner. Kim opened the small refrigerator and pulled out a container of homemade spaghetti sauce her mother had frozen and put in her packs. There were three pans under the sink and Kim chose the smallest one and dumped the sauce in it to heat. She lit the propane stove and set the pan on it. There were two burners so she put a larger pan of water on the other to boil for noodles.

There was one head of lettuce in the refrigerator. Kim figured that if she were careful she could have fresh vegetables and fruits for about the first five days of every ten-day period between deliveries. She broke enough pieces into a bowl for salad and sprinkled a little vinegar on top.

Among her small collection of books was one on edible plants in the wild. If she gained confidence in her plant-identification ability, adding a few mountain greens to her diet might be possible.

It was still warm on the catwalk so she took her dinner outside and sat in one of the two chairs on the main observation platform. When done, she wiped off her plate and bowl and put them in the sink. She had already decided she would wash dishes once a day to conserve water. She filled the one unused pan with water and put some pinto beans to soak. There'd be Mexican food tomorrow!

She grabbed one of her mother's chocolate chip cookies and went back outside to eat it. The entire sky had become a palette of sunset colors.

"Now this is living," Kim said to the world below. But the truth was that she already felt lonely. She found herself looking at her watch seeing how long it was until her nine o'clock schedule with Marc. It would be good to hear his voice, but unlike their long QSOs (conversations) of the past, she would have to limit the time to conserve batteries.

A rustling in the brush down below the lookout caught her attention. She stood up and moved quietly to the railing and was rewarded by the sight of a doe with her fawn by her side. The mother turned to look at Kim and then the two of them vanished silently into the underbrush. A chipmunk ran up the side of the platform and sat looking expectantly at Kim.

"Oh, hungry are you? Did the lookout last year feed you and you've got a good memory?"

Kim ignored the small animal for a few minutes but then reluctantly broke her cookie in two and laid a piece on the railing.

"Now I've done it for sure," she said as the chipmunk happily sat on his haunches and nibbled the treat daintily.

"I expect you'll be here for breakfast, lunch, and dinner. Just don't bring your relatives."

As the sun dropped below the horizon, the temperature dropped rapidly. Kim grabbed a sweatshirt from her duffel bag and connected her two-meter rig to the outside antenna. Time to talk to Marc.

"KA7ITR from KA7SJP."

"KA7SJP from KA7ITR—how's it going Kim?"

Kim looked at her watch. She was only going to allow herself ten minutes on the air, but there was so much to tell. Eagerly, she told Marc in detail about her setup, about the smoke reporting, the deer, the chipmunk, and how she was feeling just a little bit lonely right now.

"Wish I could zip up there," Marc said. "I'm planning on hiking there for Field Day two weeks from now, but I think that's going to be the first chance. My uncle is determined to finish this apartment complex by August. That means we're working twelve hours a day every day. You should see my blisters!"

"Just think how rich you're getting!" Kim said.

"Yeah, yeah, I know—then I'll probably accuse you of wanting me for my money," Marc joked.

Kim laughed. She knew why Marc was willing to work such long hours. Equal with his love of Amateur Radio was his devotion to music. He was an accomplished bass player and was planning to attend a music festival at Sunriver in Central Oregon in August. In addition to earning college money to supplement his engineering scholarship, he had to earn enough money to pay for the music festival. So if he worked extra hours each day, he could justify being gone from work for a week.

"Are your blisters interfering with practicing?" Kim asked.

"No, they're mainly on my palms—I think my fingers are too calloused from playing bass to ever blister. But frankly, by the time we're done at night, all I want to think about is bed. I'll have to find time to get some serious work in before August or I'll be assigned last position in the bass section."

"I doubt that, Marc—you always find time for your music. In fact, I'd hate to be lined up next to your bass and have you be told you could choose only one."

"Aw, come on Kim. I'd probably take you over my old acoustic bass—now, if it were a choice of you or the new electric fretless, well, I'd have to think about that..."

"Marc!"

"You know I don't mean it!" Marc laughed. "Maybe if I make you mad, you won't have time to be lonely. Listen, same time tomorrow night?"

"Yes, sure. I guess I had better get off. 88s (love and kisses) Marc."

"I'll deliver them in person on Field Day."

"Is that a promise?"

"You bet."

"KA7ITR from KA7SJP—goodnight, Marc."

"KA7SJP from KA7ITR—sweet dreams, Kim."

Kim felt a rush of emotion at the words "sweet dreams." It was the way Marc had signed their very first radio code conversation a year ago last spring when he had talked to her while hiking in the Cascades.* The adventures that had followed in the days after and her role in saving his life had

*See *Night Signals*.

19

brought them together in a friendship that she hoped would last a lifetime. Now she would count the days until Field Day—the annual event for Amateur Radio operators when they try to see how many stations they can contact from out in the "field" using only emergency power. A location like the lookout would be perfect. Of course, Kim would be on duty—but if Marc set up near her lookout, she could watch the fun.

She gathered up the radios and took them inside safe from the dew. She placed her few remaining belongings on shelves and then got ready for bed. The entire lookout station was lined with glass windows and Kim felt uncomfortably exposed. *I suppose I could make curtains*, she thought ruefully, *but then I'd have to pull them completely out of the way every morning. Probably everyone who came to visit with me would laugh. A lookout who is afraid of forest creatures peeking in the windows.*

With the kerosene lantern still burning, she spread her sleeping bag out on top of the bunk. She put her books to read and the lantern next to the bed. There was a latch on the inside of the door, and feeling rather foolish, she walked over to fasten it.

She slipped off her outer clothes and still in her underwear and t-shirt, she brushed her teeth hastily at the sink and climbed into bed. She had brought ten paperback books—a collection of biographies, romance, and science fiction. She started on one about aliens from the future landing on a mountaintop in Colorado and making a plan to colonize the earth. It took her only seconds to wish she hadn't opened the book.

As the ship settled down on the rocky plateau, the transparent creatures ran in all directions. A black bear ambling down a path was soon devoured and absorbed. A pinkish tinge began to color the creatures' flesh. "Absorb, absorb," their brains directed them. "Become one with the earthlings!" Soon a human appeared on the path and with a hungry rush, the aliens swarmed toward it. "Absorb!"

Kim closed the book and shuddered. She snuffed out the lamp and pulled the sleeping bag over her head. What a crummy choice of reading matter. She ought to start re-reading the *Autobiography of Benjamin Franklin* which she had also brought. What was it he talked about—oh yes, the practice of virtues. Well, fearlessness would be her virtue to work on tonight. She flung back the sleeping bag and forced herself to look out the window.

Stars, stars everywhere! How come she hadn't noticed earlier?—probably because of her lantern. The entire heavens were twinkling. She had a rudimentary knowledge of basic constellations, but beyond that, the skies were a mystery. Tomorrow, she would get out her astronomy charts to start learning the geography of the universe as well as that of the Oregon Cascades.

She yawned. She hadn't realized how tired she was. The warmth of the sleeping bag soothed her tired muscles. Soon, aliens and bears and smokes faded into the recesses of her consciousness as she closed her eyes and fell asleep.

Chapter 4

In the Forest Primeval

Saturday, June 11th, 6 a.m.
In the woods near Brutus

The long night was over. Brutus rose from his bed of crushed leaves and fir needles and turned his head toward the old logging road not far from where he was chained. His keen ears detected the sound of the man's truck. The man. Food! Saliva dripped from his jaws in anticipation.

"What's your hurry?" Lenny growled as the truck bounced over a deep rut in the road.

"It's been four days since I was out here—that's the hurry," Jay, the man driving replied. "I had to make that run to Mexico. Old Brutus has probably eaten his tail or something."

"Just a dog, big deal," Lenny said, hanging onto the door handle as Jay flew over another hole in the road.

They rumbled to a stop and Jay pulled the truck into a heavy thicket of brush. Silently, the men got out of the truck. Jay grabbed a sack of kibble and a bag with some big shank bones he'd gotten from a butcher.

Brutus was watching them, tail up, eyes alert, body still. He was perfectly silent as the men approached, but the long ropes of saliva hanging from his jaws told his hunger. Jay tossed him a bone and then with Brutus occupied, he dumped a couple of pounds of kibble on the ground within the dog's reach.

"That dog gives me the creeps," Lenny said. "Doesn't even bark—those eyes—like he's some sort of werewolf or something."

Jay grunted in satisfaction.

"That's the way we want him—he's perfect for the job. Just keep your distance so you don't become part of his dinner. Now let's go see how the crop is doing."

The "crop" the men had come to inspect was sinsemilla, a narcotic more commonly known as marijuana. Originally called "hemp" and used as rope, the utilitarian purposes of marijuana became forgotten in the middle of the twentieth century when people started using it as a narcotic.

Despite repeated medical studies showing its harmful effects, many people persisted in its use. Once they experienced the narcotic effects of the plant's chemical THC (tetrahydrocannabinol), it was hard to let go. To men like Jay and Lenny, that was good news. It meant big money.

The carpet of young green plants the men had transplanted to the forest floor just weeks before appeared lush and almost picturesque. The men walked carefully along the perimeter of the field—a field that represented a potential harvest of money. At up to $300 an ounce, and with the average plant yielding a pound of "pot," the growing plants could generate a lush crop of cash on the illegal drug market.

Like many other drug dealers, Jay and Lenny had discovered that the state and national forests were often a great place to grow their "cash crop." In remote areas away from traveled trails and roads, the marijuana could be secretly grown in the protection of the forest cover. Planted on the north side of Douglas fir seedlings, the yellow green of the plants blended almost perfectly with the young trees and their shadows. And, if by chance the plot was discovered, no one could trace its ownership through land deeds.

Lenny was fairly new at the business, but Jay had done a 20-year apprenticeship in Northern California—an apprenticeship that included two five-year jail terms and the confiscation of the private land he had leased. When he was released from jail the last time, he vowed never to go back to the sunshine state. Instead, he came north to Oregon where the residents often complained about the rain but at the same time boasted of the green beauty it produced.

Jay listened to those boasts and instead of green ferns and firs, he envisioned marijuana. First, he tried to establish a territory in Southern Oregon but found the resident illegal growers there very unfriendly to the idea of someone new on their turf. With a bullet hole in his leg and a close call with a booby trap, he moved his enterprise inside. Near Medford, a huge rented barn with boarded-up windows and carefully installed gro lights seemed the perfect way to go. Perfect until the electric company, operating on a tip, wondered why he was using so much electricity.

One of his buyers spotted the police cars enroute to the rural area and telephoned Jay. Jay set the barn afire and in the confusion, escaped to the north. He met up with Lenny through some friends and, together, the two of them started scouting the wooded mountainsides to the east of Salem.

That was three years ago. They'd had two successful crops in a row. Jay figured that in a few more, especially with expansion of his business, he would have enough money cached in the woods to retire to Mexico and a life of ease.

Lenny stopped to stroke the young plants. By the end of the summer when the marijuana began to bud, each female plant had the potential of being worth two to three thousand dollars. They would keep harvesting until frost. Of course, fall was the most dangerous time too. The flowering plants could be spotted by aerial surveillance planes. Sheriff's deputies and U. S. Forest Service officials were always on the lookout for marijuana plots in the forests. When they found them, they harvested the plants and then torched them.

Often there were booby traps—everything from fish hooks hanging on monofilament fishing line to detonators and punjii sticks. Officials had to take precautionary military-like tactics before moving into a growing field that might be as dangerous as a mine field. All explosive devices had to be located and disarmed before cleanup of the plants could begin. More than one deputy and innocent hiker had been injured or even killed by stumbling across booby-trapped fields.

Jay and Lenny's security system was no exception. They had the perimeter of their operation guarded by a variety of traps. And Brutus there on a long chain should dissuade even the most hardy. One of the dog's purposes, while they were there, was to give the men more time should law enforcement officials arrive. By releasing Brutus to attack, they could buy themselves precious minutes to escape. Already, they had planned an alternate escape route should the logging road be blocked.

Now the two of them walked down to the creek running through the center of the growing field. Because of the dry spring and the potentially dry summer, they had installed plastic irrigation tubing that fed the growing seedlings with vital water. Light applications of fertilizer were encouraging the natural growth of the plants. What Jay and Lenny didn't know or care was that the runoff of fertilizer into the stream was polluting it and causing the death of many fish and animals who drank from it.

Jay kicked at a plant showing signs of drying.

"I wish we'd get some rain—where's all that famous Oregon rain when we need it?"

Lenny bent over, fashioning a drip irrigation tube from the spaghetti-thin plastic tubing. Soon, water began to trickle out on the ground around the dehydrated plants.

"That ought to help," he said with satisfaction. "As long as there aren't any fires."

Jay looked at him with alarm.

"Don't even say that word," he mumbled.

They walked over to look at the creek. Normally, a rushing stream, this year its banks were way above water level. Rocks that were usually submerged sat three-fourths of the way out of the water. Jay looked up at the sunlight glinting down between the towering firs.

"Man, it's hot," he said, wiping his sweaty, unshaven face with a bandana. "I don't ever remember a June this hot. I was going to put up the camouflage netting today, but I think we'll wait until next week. Don't really need it yet, anyway. But, we do need to put more irrigation tubes in that patch over there, and I didn't bring enough—guess we'll have to come back tomorrow night."

"No way!" Lenny protested. "I had plans for tomorrow — gonna meet that redhead down at the tavern."

"Don't worry," Jay said sarcastically. "We'll come up here around dinnertime, and you'll be back home before dark—when all the action starts. And, just make sure you don't start talking when you start drinking. I don't want to get anybody curious about what we're doing."

After Brutus had finished eating, Jay walked over and turned the muscular dog loose. He stopped to drink at the stream and then turned toward the men.

Lenny froze as Brutus ran back and forth with his nose to the ground. He passed behind Lenny's legs but didn't even stop to sniff. Instead he went into the brush to take care of his needs.

"Why'd you let him go?" Lenny whispered.

Jay laughed.

"He won't hurt you unless I tell him to—just wanted to let him stretch his legs a little—you know, keep him happy on the job."

Lenny stood perfectly still until Jay whistled for the dog and had him safely back on his chain. He gave him the rest of the bones, filled a bucket of water, and then motioned for Lenny to get in the truck.

"I don't like this—coming out here in broad daylight. Supposin' someone sees us," Lenny said as Jay drove the truck to the logging road where it joined with the main highway.

Just then, a truck full of Douglas fir logs drove by, and the driver waved at Jay waiting to cross onto the road.

"See what I mean," Lenny complained.

"Forget it," Jay said. "He probably waves at everyone he sees. "Nobody's going to notice us."

"Yeah? Well, how about when we start hauling the stuff out—how 'bout then?"

"Same as last year," Jay reassured him. We build up our false load of firewood on the other truck with the hidden hollow in the middle. Just load the plants in, plop a few more logs on top for effect and drive it on out. I'll even buy firewood permits like I did last year so if anyone stops us, it looks legitimate."

"Where are we going to store it?—seeing as Mel sold that place we lived at last year," Lenny asked.

"Oh, I forgot to tell you, partner. We're moving next week, so pack up your bags, your yellow rubber ducky, and anything else you want to take. I found a farm to lease in Silverton—has an ancient barn out back—doesn't look like it's got too many years left, but it'll serve our purposes fine for this one."

"Thanks for telling me, Jay," Lenny said, frowning—"It's like you don't trust me or something—you make all the plans and I find out about them as they happen."

"You complaining about how much money you made last year, Len?"

There was silence. Then a quieter voice.

"No, I guess not."

"You'll like this place, Lenny. Even has its own pond. And there's room to put up three plastic greenhouses next year so we can grow both inside and out."

Lenny's eyes grew big as he calculated what this new idea of Jay's might mean in terms of money. He smiled as he looked out the window. The sun was completely up now and the hay fields, almost ready to be harvested, glistened in the early morning dew.

Because of the unseasonable heat, not only the hay but the strawberry harvest was also a full two weeks early. Truckloads of workers were arriving in the strawberry fields bordering the highway. Lenny watched as the pickers, mostly kids, got off the buses and carried picking baskets into the fields.

He mentally compared what he was making off the marijuana to what the pickers would make for a day's wages harvesting berries under the hot sun. The thought made his previous smile turn to a grin. But what increased his happiness even more was the thought of many of the young pickers becoming potential customers for his product.

"You know, Jay," he reflected. "What we need are more customers. Maybe we ought to start advertising in the *Wall Street Journal* or something."

Jay snorted in amusement. He reached over and punched Lenny lightly on the shoulder.

"That's what I like about you, Lenny. You're always good for a laugh."

Chapter 5

First Day on Duty

Saturday, June 11th
Vista Peak Lookout

Kim looked at her watch and groaned. 5:00 a.m.! But there was no denying the early morning light pouring into her glass home. She rubbed her eyes and turned on her side to gaze out the windows at the valleys shrouded with ground fog. A lone hawk circling above the forest swooped into the mist and then rose again into the sunshine.

"Probably can't spot its breakfast through that stuff," Kim said aloud. "Eating mice at the crack of dawn—ugh!"

She sat up and shivered. The air felt icy. Quickly, she jumped out of bed and lit the fire she had laid in the woodstove the night before. Picking up the binoculars, she gave a quick scan in all directions. All looked peaceful in the valley, so she returned to the sleeping bag. Kim rubbed her cold feet against each other as the comforting sound of the crackling fire gave both physical and emotional warmth to the room.

The lookout seemed entirely different to her this morning than it had last night. No more imagined creatures peering in through the dark windows at her. No more ghostly images bouncing in the wind-tossed fir trees. Now it was a peaceful cabin, very much like a large dorm room with a view.

She reached over the side of the bunk and pulled a pair of jeans and sweatshirt up into the sleeping bag with her. By wiggling around, she managed to get completely dressed without ever getting out of bed. By the time she was done, the room was warm from the fire. She set her pot of pinto beans on the woodstove surface to simmer throughout the day.

Slipping her feet into tennis shoes, Kim reluctantly got up and put a kettle of water on to boil on the stove. While it was heating, she combed her hair and made a quick trip down the trail to the outhouse.

"Brrr," she said, rubbing her arms as she ran back up the trail to the welcome warmth of her new home. The tea-kettle was singing, and Kim poured a small amount of hot water into a basin to wash. The rest she poured into a flowered mug with a peppermint tea bag and into a bowl of instant oatmeal. She sliced a banana on the hot cereal and sat down to eat by the fire.

Last night, she had started a list of things to do. Now she added more to it.

1. Get physically fit—hike! Exercise!
2. Write letters
3. Work DX (far away stations)
4. Study for Advanced Class amateur license
5. Knit sweater
6. Study astronomy
7. Work DX
8. Work DX.

"Hmmm, I seem to be hung up on that idea," she laughed aloud. She looked over at "Jessie," her dark gray transceiver connected to the antenna that Jack had helped her string. Tonight, she would try it out after a full day of charging the solar cells.

Breakfast over, dishes in the sink, she tidied her small home, and moved out on the deck for her first intensive scan of the mountains for the day. The fog was lifting. It was going to be a clear day after all. Some noisy blue jays were chasing the circling hawk away from the trees. Probably guarding their nest.

She set up the forest radio and its microphone on the small table on the deck so she could hear any calls while she was outside. Sure enough, there was House Mountain reporting a smoke due north of them. Kim grabbed her binoculars and scanned the terrain. A small wisp of smoke was curling skyward—definitely much closer to the House Mountain lookout than to her. She ran inside to sight it with her fire finder and then called in her azimuth. She wished she had seen it first.

Kim puttered around inside the lookout, tidying up her belongings. Promptly at fifteen minutes after the hour, she went outside to do her quarter-hour scan. By noon, she found it was no longer necessary to look at her watch. Her brain had become adept at judging fifteen-minute intervals, and she automatically moved from inside to outside.

She watched the progress of a slash burn that the lookouts had been advised was underway. Slash burns were used to destroy residue from logging—to kill insects, to make way for fresh new growth, and to prevent a future catastrophic forest fire. The light gray and white clouds of smoke which had looked ominous at first were definitely subsiding—evidence that the burn was being carefully controlled.

Lunch on the deck was another banana and some crackers with cheese. The chipmunk joined her immediately, but Kim was hungry so she made him settle for just a few crumbs. She leaned her head back against the lookout wall. The sun was warm and soothing. She had to be careful she didn't go to sleep.

"Hello?"

Kim jumped at the voice. A young man and woman close to her own age were at the bottom of the stairs.

"Hi. I didn't hear you. Come on up," she welcomed them.

"Thanks. My name's Bill Koppler and this is Theresa Greenley."

They all shook hands. Kim asked them where they were from, and Bill said they both lived in Portland.

"I met your friend, Marc, at a ham club meeting there, and he told me about your lookout position and the fact that he was coming up for Field Day. My call sign is W6ANX."

Kim's eyes grew wide with surprise.

"You mean—you're amateurs too—this is incredible. First the packer, then a couple in another lookout, and you, my first visitors—all ham radio operators. I knew there were a lot of us—over a million and a half worldwide, but it looks like this area is particularly blessed."

"Blessed?" Theresa questioned, laughing.

"Yeah, blessed—that's the right word," Bill said grinning at her. "You see," he explained to Kim, "Theresa isn't one of us yet." The way he said "one of us" made it sound like some secret society.

Theresa laughed again. "I've only known Bill for a couple of months, and he's talked nonstop about this wonderful hobby of his. I think I'm well on my way to becoming hooked, but I don't have a license yet."

"Which is part of the reason we came to see you," Bill explained. "I want Theresa to see a Field Day in operation. Marc kind of unofficially asked the club if we'd like to set up here. He's going to talk about it to you on the air, but Theresa and I wanted to go hiking today anyway, so I thought we'd come up here to see you. Would you mind being invaded by about ten eager Field Day enthusiasts?"

"Well, no, I don't mind—but you must tell everyone to bring his own drinking water and supplies. I'm very limited as to what I have."

"Yeah, Marc already told us that."

"He did, huh?" Kim laughed. "It might be nice if he'd tell me what he's planning!"

"Don't be mad at him," Bill said. "He called me last night right after he talked to you—said he felt awful that he had forgotten to mention it. Said he was just so blown away by the beauty of your voice on the air..."

"Uh huh," Kim said, smiling. "Don't worry, I'll forgive him. I always forgive Marc. Oops—it's one o'clock—time to do my check."

Bill and Theresa sat down comfortably in the warm sun while Kim walked around the perimeter of the deck checking the horizon in all directions.

"You know, I think you probably should check with the Forestry Department before you bring that many people up here for a night," Kim said.

"You're right. In fact, we already stopped at the Ranger Station and asked," Theresa replied. "They said no problem as long as we didn't build any fires and as long as we set up far enough away from you so as not to be a distraction."

"You could use that knoll over there," Kim said, pointing at a small rise a couple of hundred yards away.

She stopped talking suddenly and stared off the east deck. A plume of gray smoke was wafting up from the bottom of one of the canyons.

"Excuse me!" Kim said as she ran inside to get an azimuth on the smoke. Seconds later, she was back and grabbed the microphone.

"Willamette Dispatch, this is Vista Peak."

"Go ahead, Vista Peak."

Triumphantly, Kim recited the exact location of the spotted smoke. Almost immediately, a second lookout called in a cross shot, confirming her coordinates. A few minutes or so after the center acknowledged the sighting, the voice of the second lookout who had cross sighted the smoke came on the air.

"Nice job, Vista Peak—you beat me."

"Who's this?" Kim asked.

"High Camp—name's Joe. Welcome to the crew."

"Hi, Joe. My name's Kim. Thank you."

Kim expected the conversation to continue but it didn't. She turned back to her guests and explained.

"We're not supposed to talk much on the radio except for business," Kim said, sitting down on the bench by Theresa. "You can't believe how good that makes me feel to call that in first. I missed two smokes this morning. I guess no one thought I was even here."

Bill was standing on the south side of the lookout, two-meter rig in hand, his face covered with a big grin.

Theresa looked at Kim quizzically.

"What's he so happy about?" she asked.

"He's doing the same thing I did yesterday afternoon—from this elevation above the mountaintops, you can reach every repeater in the Willamette Valley."

Bill motioned for Theresa to come join him. Soon he was introducing her to amateurs he was talking to in Bend, Salem,

Albany, Silverton, and even one mobile operator driving along the Santiam Highway.

Yes, she's hooked, thought Kim, remembering the thrill she'd felt the first time she was introduced to someone on the radio and discovered that the magic of shortwaves could help her make friends all over the world.

Kim picked up her binoculars and made her quarterly scan. All was quiet. The slash burn was out, just a few wisps of smoke remaining. Bill had turned off his radio and was putting it away in his backpack.

"Wow!—that's all I can say is wow!"

"Yes, I know it's addictive," Kim agreed. "If it weren't for having to conserve my batteries, I would have stayed on to all hours last night. Now, I'm looking forward to working some DX tonight on the big rig. By the way, would you two like to stay for dinner? I'm attempting Mexican food."

"Thanks, Kim," Theresa said. "Wish we could, but we need to get back to Portland. We're going out to dinner with some friends there."

"Dinner—that reminds me," Bill said, reaching into his backpack. "Marc would have killed me if I had forgotten to give you this."

He handed Kim a parcel neatly wrapped in foil. She laid it on the table and pulled back the wrapping. Inside were four rosy peaches, a bag of pistachio nuts, a big square of milk chocolate, and three cans of root beer.

"Ooh, he knows all my weaknesses. Gee, I'd better put the chocolate in the refrigerator. It feels kind of soft. I was going to live on a spartan diet up here, and my mother sends me off with chocolate chip cookies and now these treats. Not that I'm complaining," Kim laughed.

She stowed her treasures and then walked to the bottom of the stairs with Theresa and Bill.

"Sorry, I can't go farther with you, but it's just about time to do a scan again. I'm so glad to meet you both, and I'll be looking forward to Field Day," Kim said holding out her hand.

They shook hands, and Kim watched them as they walked down the trail. She smiled as she saw Bill looking at the trees on the knoll for the prospective Field Day site, knowing he was mentally stringing antennas. They turned to wave at Kim and then disappeared around the bend. Kim climbed the stairs back to the lookout tower and resumed her watch.

Surprisingly, the afternoon hours flew by. She found herself so occupied with thoughts of Field Day that it seemed like the quarter hours almost merged. Soon, it was six o'clock. She went inside. The beans were done perfectly. Kim took a big fork and mashed them against the sides of the kettle.

Earlier in the afternoon, she had wrapped a few tortillas in the foil Marc's gift had come in. They had been toasting in the sunshine for three hours. She scooped some beans into the center of each one, added a little of her precious cheese and lettuce, and took them and a cold root beer out on the deck. The chipmunk was there immediately, this time with another slightly smaller one.

"Oh, brought your wife did you? Or is that your son or daughter? Cousin?"

The chipmunks twitched their tails as they ran back and forth on the railing waiting for the expected handout. Kim didn't disappoint them.

"This is getting serious, you know. If you bring the entire chipmunk population up here, we're going to have to have a talk. Can't you just keep this little arrangement quiet?"

Two sets of beady eyes stared back at Kim promising whatever she wanted to read into them.

"Okay, you guys—that's it. Go on back to your homes. I'll see you in the morning, I'm sure."

She stood up to take her root beer can back inside, and the two disappeared obediently over the side of the deck. Kim put the pot of beans in the refrigerator.

"Made a few more than I thought," she laughed aloud. "Looks like beans all week."

As soon as the kitchen was tidy, she locked the lookout, slipped the key in her pocket, and set off down the trail leading to the east. Kim had promised herself she would explore a new direction each evening. She knew she was out of shape, but hopefully within a few weeks, she would work up to a four- or five-mile hike each night. With the late sunsets and extended twilight, she would have plenty of time to explore and still get back in time for an hour or so of radio time before going to bed.

Despite the day's heat, the evening air felt soft. She stopped to admire some dewberry bushes in bloom. In spite of the drought, the flowers promised berries later in the summer. Thinking about all the happenings of the day, Kim walked along the trail under the canopy of fir trees.

After walking for about an hour, she was just getting ready to turn around when the sound of running water intrigued her. A stream must be close by. She found an opening in the blackberry bushes and eased her way through the brush toward the sound. At the bottom of an embankment, a shallow stream rippled over rocks in a wide creek bed that obviously was used to more water.

The water looked inviting, and Kim considered taking off her shoes and wading. But the lure of hearing far-away radio signals seemed more important at the moment, so reluctantly she turned back toward the trail. Just then a flash of silver caught her eye. A few yards downstream several dead fish were lying at the water's edge. She walked over to investigate. Rainbow trout. Odd. She turned them over with a stick. They looked like young healthy fish, but then of course, what did she know?

The sky was definitely getting darker. Kim hurried back up the trail and half jogged to the lookout. It was almost 9 p.m. when she got there. Time for her contact with Marc on two meters. He was there as she expected. Happily, she told him of the day's events and her visitors. Fifteen minutes later, they said goodnight. Kim laid a sweatshirt across her shoulders for warmth and then settled down at "Jessie."

The transceiver tuned up beautifully, and with great anticipation, Kim depressed the push to talk button on her microphone.

"CQ, CQ, CQ — CQ 20 meters—this is KA7SJP, King, Alfa, Seven, Sierra, John, Papa, calling CQ and standing by."

"KA7SJP, this is KG6ASP in Guam returning your call. I'm hearing you 5/4 here at the Naval Communications Station in Guam. Name here is Gary. How do you copy me?"

Kim let out a whoop of joy. Guam on her very first try! What a summer this was going to be!

Chapter 6

Stranger on the Trail

Sunday, June 12th, 6 p.m.

"Here," Jay said angrily. "Hold this tubing while I punch some more holes. Hey! I said hold this—what are you gaping at anyway?"

He glared up at Lenny who was gazing at a rocky slope about a hundred yards from the marijuana.

"Oh! I'm sorry—here, let me take that stuff. I was just thinking that would make a good place to do a little plinking with the .22."

"Forget it, Lenny—we got work to do."

The two of them bent over their task. Lenny held the thin plastic tubing while Jay punched holes in the main irrigation lines and attached the feeder tubes. Soon, water was trickling out amongst the thirsty plants.

"We done?" Lenny asked impatiently.

"Just about," Jay answered. "But I want to sit here for a half hour or so and make sure that the flow is right. If it starts getting too wet, I want to remove some of the tubes. Why don't you go take a hike or something—only leave that gun behind!"

"Ah, Jay—never know—I might run into a four point buck or something—venison for dinner!" He grinned at his scowling partner.

"Sure, Lenny, sure—deer hunting in June—wonder how far we'd get down the mountain with a carcass tied on the truck."

Lenny laughed and left, the rifle over his shoulder. Jay watched him disappear up the trail and shook his head. He was beginning to have second thoughts about this partner of his who had seemed so eager.

What he was really wondering was if Lenny was operating with a full deck in the brain department. Be like him to meet a forest ranger on the trail and shoot him. Jay lit a cigarette and thought some more about the blond, disheveled man he'd hooked up with. The summer would be over before they knew it, and if Lenny proved to be too much trouble, he'd tell him in no uncertain terms to get walking. He sat down on the ground and leaned up against the rough trunk of a fir tree to watch the water wind its way through the plants.

* * * * * * * *

Kim dried her plate and the pan she had heated dinner in and put them both away in the cupboard. Quickly, she donned hiking shoes and put her two-meter radio and a small water bottle in a light backpack. Another successful day on the job! This was beginning to feel great. Admittedly, her legs felt a little stiff from the unaccustomed hiking, but she told herself that would soon change.

She locked the lookout and slipped the key into her pocket, taking in the beautiful view of Mt. Hood, Mt. Adams, Mt. Jefferson, and the volcanic Mt. St. Helens. They were all magnificent companions.

"Hmmm, let's see," said Kim, considering her trail choices—I think I'll go this way tonight," she said aloud, picking a different trail from the night before.

She set off jauntily down the trail, inhaling the sweet night dusk air, and listening to the calls of birds high in the trees. A chipmunk ran down the trail ahead of her.

"Oh, are you coming along too? Is it you?—or one of your relatives?"

The small creature turned to look at her and then disappeared under a rock. Kim plucked a huckleberry blossom from an overhanging vine. The flower was shriveling in the heat and drought.

"I doubt anyone's going to get berries out of these," Kim said sadly. "And I was planning on huckleberry pie."

Her shoes kicked up small puffs of dust on the dry trail as she wound her way deeper into the cover of the woods. Suddenly, gunshots rang out! Kim froze as the possibilities ran through her mind. It wasn't hunting season—she knew that. Who could be shooting? And at what? She turned to go back up the trail.

Oh relax, Kim, she told herself. *It's probably somebody target practicing. If you're going to get spooked by everything you hear, you'll never last the summer.* She thought ruefully of her fear while reading the science fiction book that first night and smiled at herself.

"First thing you know, I'll be seeing aliens from outer space on the trail," she said aloud.

But there was someone on the trail. She heard twigs breaking under his footsteps before she actually saw him. She paused, uncertain what to do. She started to reach for the radio in her backpack, but before she had even unzipped the pack, a tall, blond unshaven man in a tank top and cutoffs came around the bend in the trail. He shouldered a .22 rifle and seemed startled when he saw Kim.

"Hi," she said, in what she hoped was a voice that implied nonchalance at meeting an armed man in the woods.

He stared at her for a moment and then grunted, "Hi."

Their eyes locked in silence. Kim felt nervous sweat dripping down between her shoulder blades.

"Hot, isn't it?" she said weakly.

"Who are you?" the man asked gruffly.

"The fire lookout," she said, pointing vaguely back up the trail. "Just going for an after dinner hike before I ... before I meet with the others." *He doesn't have to know that I meet with them on the air,* she thought. Somehow it seemed very important to make this man think she wasn't alone in the lookout.

"Well, you oughtn't to go out walking by yourself," the man grumbled. "Ought to stay up there in your lookout and do your job."

Before Kim could say anything, he turned and disappeared back down the trail. She stood silently, waiting for her heart to slow to its normal speed.

She pulled the two-meter rig out of her backpack. She wasn't sure if she could contact anyone since she was behind the crest of the hill, but just for reassurance, she turned it on. To her surprise, she heard a conversation between a ham in Sisters and her lookout friend, Alyse, N7NYJ. She waited until they had signed and then called Alyse. Keeping her voice low, she spoke into the microphone.

"N7NYJ from KA7SJP—hi, Alyse."

"Well hi, Kim—are you at the lookout?"

"Well, actually, no—I'm on a trail about a half hour from the lookout."

"Are you okay? You sound kind of out of breath or something."

"Yes, I'm okay—I uh ... I just ran into kind of a creepy guy on the trail—carrying a .22—told me I ought to stay in the lookout."

Alyse sounded concerned.

"Do you want me to come over there and spend the night with you?" she asked.

"No, I'm okay, really I am. He went the other way—out target practicing, I think. I can't let everyone I meet freak me out."

"Tell you what, Kim," Alyse said. "Call me again as soon as you get back to the lookout and how about again at 10?"

"Sure," Kim agreed. She was already beginning to feel better as she neared the crest of the trail near the lookout. The sunset was magnificent.

"I'm sure I'm just over-imagining things," she told Alyse. Then she told her about her mistake in choosing bedtime reading on Friday night, and they both had a good laugh before signing off.

* * * * * * * *

"I don't know," Alyse said, turning to her husband, Frank, in the Coffin Mountain Lookout. "Do you think I should go over there?"

"Well, I worry about the girls who are alone, but Alyse you know nothing's ever happened to any of them. If one of us goes over there, we'll probably scare her more—make her even more afraid of every stranger she meets. Let's just check with her by radio tonight."

"Okay, I guess you're right," Alyse said. "Still, it's hard not to worry."

* * * * * * * *

Although Kim locked the door of the lookout from the inside, she really did forget about the stranger after she checked in with Frank and Alyse. Marc was going to be at a movie tonight with his family so for once she wouldn't have a 9 p.m. schedule with him. She reminded herself to check back with her friends at Coffin Mountain at 10 and then sat down at "Jessie" to work DX.

Tonight was particularly good. She talked to a maritime mobile station, a couple sailing a yacht from Hawaii to San Diego. And then after that, Japan rolled in like gangbusters. Kim had to write fast to copy down all of her contacts in her log. Soon, her allotted hour of battery time was up, so she shut off the rig.

She got ready for bed and climbed in the bunk. The tiredness of her muscles overrode her imagination and she was soon asleep.

* * * * * * * *

"You said we'd be home by dark," Lenny grumbled as the aging pickup struggled over potholes in the forestry road.

"Yeah, well you're the one who was so stupid to go firing that gun after I told you not too. What were you doing anyway?"

"Just shooting at some beer cans," Lenny said.

"We're not the only ones in these woods, dumbhead—you want to bring in the posse?"

"Sorry," Lenny mumbled. "You're right about not being the only ones—I met a girl on the trail."

Jay was instantly alert.

"A girl? A girl from where?"

"Said she was a lookout—I told her not to go out walking around."

"You what? Now you probably made her curious—you really are as dumb as you look," Jay said, shaking his head in disgust.

"Oh, big deal," Lenny said. "She was just out taking a hike. I think I scared her—she probably won't go down that trail again."

"She better not," Jay said in a low voice. "The last thing I want to have to do is dispose of some dumb girl."

Lenny looked at Jay but then decided the subject was closed.

"Step on it, will ya'? That redhead's probably not going to wait for me all night."

* * * * * * * *

Sunday, 11 p.m.
In a tavern near Salem

The woman with red hair had waited for Lenny, but it took only about ten minutes of his foul language and unkempt appearance before she left the tavern. Jay, watching the unsuccessful romantic endeavors of Lenny, laughed aloud.

"I told you to take a bath before you came here," Jay said. "But no, you just slicked your hair back and tucked your shirt in. No wonder she left. You smell like a billy goat."

Lenny glowered at Jay but he knew better than to swing at him. Instead, he turned his back and resumed drinking his beer. Jay walked over to the pool table and started a game with another man. Pretty soon, a rough-looking individual wearing dirty jeans, a plaid shirt and red suspenders came over and sat down by Lenny.

"That your friend over there?" he said, gesturing at Jay.

"Yeah, what about it?" Lenny grunted.

"He shouldn'ta talked to you that way—he's pretty ugly himself. In fact, he's uglier than a cockroach."

"Yeah, well trouble is, you're even uglier and dumb!" Lenny said, turning away. Instantly, a hand grabbed him and whirled him around.

"Whadya' mean, ugly? Dumb?" he snarled. "Look pal, my girlfriend don't think so, and besides that, I'm gonna be rich come fall—just as soon as my pot crop's all sold."

"Pot? humpf?—you think you gotta crop—why me and my buddy, we're real farmers. Right up in the woods here," Lenny said proudly.

Lenny never felt Jay's hands as they picked him up and propelled him out the door. Angrily, Jay shoved Lenny toward their pickup.

"Moron—I can't believe you—why don't you just call up the cops and tell them what we're growing or take an ad out in the yellow pages? You must not have any brains at all!"

"I'm sorry, boss," Lenny mumbled. He started to walk to the truck but was having trouble.

Jay grabbed him by the back of his belt and shoved him into the truck.

"A lizard's got more sense than you," Jay said as they roared out of the parking lot.

Chapter 7

Field Day

Saturday, June 25th
Vista Peak Lookout

Kim felt almost like a veteran as she quickly dressed on the morning of June 25th. The last two weeks had seasoned her into a "real lookout." The competitive eagerness that marked the way she tackled all projects had soon made her proficient at locating smokes and calling them in quickly. The landscape was becoming as familiar to her as her own backyard in Salem.

Too, she had adapted well to her mountain routine. Now, five pounds lighter and suntanned, she found herself waking eagerly at each new dawn. The days swept by quickly—a blur of scanning the horizon, talking to the chipmunks and an occasional human visitor, and housekeeping duties.

She had even become used to being away from the conveniences of home. The solar shower bag filled with water warmed by the sunshine was a treat she allowed herself twice a week. In between, she kept clean with sponge baths taken each morning with water she heated on the stove. So far, she hadn't tried skinny-dipping in the stream. She was painfully aware of the need to conserve water—so much so that on his first resupply visit this last week, Jack had whistled at the amount she had left.

"It's okay to take a drink once in a while, Kim," he joked.

So now, she was being a little less frugal. In fact, as soon as she was dressed this morning, she put a large jar of sun tea out on the deck to steep. When it was made, she planned on having one of the Field Day participants hike down to put it in the stream to chill.

Of all the day's activities the past two weeks, Kim found that she looked forward to evenings the most. She ate rapidly each night so she could go hiking. A four-mile radius from the lookout had already been explored, and as her trail endurance increased, she planned on extending the circle another couple of miles. Every night, she walked for an hour and then turned homeward. The trip back was usually made in 45 minutes even though it was uphill. That was because Kim knew what waited for her: first a heartfelt QSO with Marc on two meters and then the world on twenty meters.

A log by "Jessie" was testimony to her contacts. South Africa, Ecuador, Japan, Russia. Every night, some fresh part of the world rolled in over the airwaves, and Kim happily talked to new-found friends. This last Thursday night had been a special treat. ZL1CBO, a sheep rancher in New Zealand, had come back to her call. Then he had put his wife, ZL1TPZ, and his teenaged daughter, ZL1TNM, on the air. An hour later when her power started to fade, Kim had reluctantly signed with them.

She definitely planned to write a letter to this New Zealand family. These were friends she wanted to keep for a lifetime. Someday, if all her travel fantasies came true, she would travel to New Zealand and meet them in person.

Kim rubbed her eyes. She hadn't gotten to bed until nearly midnight. Marc and nine other radio operators had trudged the three-mile trail up the mountain Friday evening to set up for today's Field Day. Kim had spotted their cars the minute they turned off the main road and parked at the trailhead. She was still on duty when they arrived. Marc must have told everyone that she couldn't spend much time talking to them until after 6 p.m. She saw them plop down their equipment on the knoll. Her first instinct was to run greet them, but it was 5:45—time for another scan.

She'd had her back to the group, scanning the south, when a familiar voice made her jump. She turned to see Marc standing at the foot of the steps.

"Permission to come aboard, Captain?" he asked, his brown eyes twinkling.

"Permission granted," Kim laughed.

Then he vaulted the steps, gathered her in his arms, and whirled her around much to the amusement and cheers of the rest of the group watching.

"Oh, go string an antenna or something," Marc shouted. He grabbed her hand to lead her behind the lookout and then laughed at all the glass windows.

"Boy, there's no place to hide up here, is there?"

"No," agreed Kim, laughing.

Marc turned so that his back was to the group and bent to kiss her. The group actually was stringing antennas by now, so there was no applause.

"Hi," Marc said softly.

"Hi, yourself," Kim said. "You look great."

"You look better than great," Marc said. "You look beautiful!"

"Even with my sunburned nose?" Kim teased.

Marc kissed the tip of her nose.

"There," he said. "Now it won't burn anymore. I just put my magic spell on it. Say! Are you off duty now? I don't want to be standing between you and the safety of the forest."

"Just off, right now," Kim said. "Perfect timing."

"Well, come on, I want you to meet the group," Marc said, grabbing her hand.

The two of them walked down the trail and up the hillside leading to the grassy knoll topped with several fir trees. The other amateurs were all busy—hooking up the various transceivers to battery packs and stringing antennas. Kim smiled at the sight. She knew that all over the United States, this scene was being enacted in fields, backyards, parks, mountaintops, rooftops—anywhere that a group of hams decided to participate in the annual contest known as "Field Day."

There were several categories of competition depending upon the number of operators and the equipment used. But the basic principle was the same: operate on emergency power for no more than 24 hours to demonstrate the usefulness of Amateur Radio communications in a real emergency. The goal was to make as many contacts as possible and for the next day and night, the airwaves would be jammed with the call, "CQ Field Day."

Marc led Kim through the group, introducing her to each person.

"This is Richard, KA7OZO, president of our club."

"Hi, Kim—thanks for letting us use your spot in paradise here."

"Hi, Richard. It belongs to you as much as to me. We're all taxpayers. I'm glad to have the company."

They shook hands and Kim and Marc moved on to the edge of the gathering. Kim recognized Theresa, who was busily cooking stew on a Coleman stove. An attractive young Afro-American woman with a radiant smile was standing next to her chatting.

"Hi, Theresa," Kim said. "How come they've got you cooking instead of stringing wire?"

Theresa looked up and laughed.

"I guess that's one of the penalties of not having a license," she said. "But Bill has promised me that when they get started, I'll be in the thick of things. Kim and Marc, I want you to meet my friend, Heather. We knew each other in high school, and she's out to the Northwest for a visit. In fact, she rode her motorcycle all the way across the country—how's that for a mobile station?"

Heather laughed while Theresa continued her praise.

"I convinced her to come to Field Day with us. Oops, what's your call, Heather?—I know you amateurs always introduce each other by your call letters. Sometimes I wonder if you have names."

"Hi," said Heather, shaking hands with Kim and Marc. "The call's N3CUD—I'm certainly enjoying your beautiful country. In fact, of every state I've ridden through, this is the greenest."

"There's a reason for that," Kim laughed. "We joke about rust, mildew, and slugs here in Oregon—all the rain! But unfortunately this year, there hasn't been much. I'm afraid we may turn into a brown state instead of a green one if Mother Nature doesn't kick in soon. Anyway, I'm glad you're here."

And so the evening had continued. The group had brought plenty of food—enough so, as Marc put it—"We can leave Kim with some goodies." They ate bowls of hot stew that tasted good in the cool evening air. Then it was back to work.

The major operating station had been set up, but Kim watched as Marc opened up a knapsack and pulled out a familiar-looking piece of gear. It was his small seven-pound battery-powered HW-9 transceiver, the same piece of gear that had saved his life the previous summer.*

"You're kidding," Kim said. "You never told me you finally fixed it."

"Good as new," Marc said beaming. "I vowed I'd never go hiking without it again, and I even brought along a flashlight—just in case," he laughed.

Kim shook her head. It was still hard to believe that the rig had sent out signals with nine volts from those flashlight batteries instead of the required twelve. But it had—the fact that Marc was alive was proof of that.

Everyone followed Kim over to the lookout to stow extra food in her refrigerator. They sat for awhile on the deck, swapping stories. But then at close to midnight, Kim stood up.

"Sorry you guys, but I'm a working girl—have to be on duty officially at 9 in the morning, but I always like to start watching much earlier than that. So I'm afraid I need to get some sleep."

"And we want to be on the air," said Richard. "Early bird gets the DX."

"Or something like that," said Marc.

"Actually, we can't start transmitting for the contest until 11 a.m.," Bill explained to Theresa, "but we can talk to people for fun before that."

The group departed, considerately leaving Marc alone to tell Kim goodnight.

*See *Night Signals.*

"Of course if I take more than five minutes, they'll show me no mercy," Marc told her.

"That's okay, you're tough—right?" Kim said kissing him gently.

But they soon said goodnight, promising to spend as much time as possible together the next two days. Kim crawled into bed and within seconds was fast asleep.

Now it was morning. 5 a.m. Smiling as she relived the events of the night before, Kim quickly made herself breakfast. She wouldn't really have time to visit the group until nighttime. She was hoping that they would take turns coming over to see her. In the meantime, she wanted to try making a special treat for their dinner tonight. She had asked Jack to bring her up some baking apples on his last visit, and he had complied with a dozen beautiful pippins.

Her mother had given him a sealed container of premixed pie dough, rolled out and then re-rolled in wax paper. Now, Kim hastily looked through the cupboard. A pie pan! There was no pie pan. Why hadn't she thought of that?

She paced the floor thinking. Suddenly, she had it. There were two metal ice cube trays in the freezer compartment of her small propane refrigerator. She transferred the precious cubes to a plastic bowl and lined the trays with pie dough. Deftly, she sliced the apples into the trays and covered them with cinnamon and sugar and the rest of the pie dough. The completed mini pies went into a big Dutch oven on the stove.

By the time, she had finished her first lookout duty of the day, the aroma of freshly baked apple pies filled the air.

"Yum, what's that I smell?" Marc and Bill and Theresa and Heather were at the foot of the stairs.

"Apple pie—sort of," Kim said. "You know, I was planning it for dinner, but I bet it would go great with morning coffee."

"I bet it would too," said Marc sniffing the air appreciatively.

"Okay—grab something to carry them in—they're hot, and tell everyone I send greetings. I really can't leave here, so just ask people to visit me when they can. I'd like to know how you're doing with Field Day."

Bill and Theresa and Heather left, carrying the pies carefully. Marc settled down in a deck chair.

"I can't stay long—we want to start testing equipment soon, but I just wanted to make sure you were as beautiful in the morning as you were last night."

"And?" Kim said smiling.

"Even more so," Marc said.

Just then there was a yell of "Hey Marc—we could use you over here." Reluctantly, he got up to leave.

"I shall return—that's a promise."

"You'd better," said Kim.

It was noon before Marc managed a few minutes away. Kim listened to him report the long list of stations contacted. They were doing exceedingly well.

"Bill had Theresa on the mike a few minutes ago. After she finished talking to a station in Argentina, she asked us if anyone had brought a license manual along—she wants to start studying right now!"

Kim laughed. "That's the way it was for me too—except my first contact was with Santa—my Uncle Steve arranged the whole thing."

"So that's why you were so determined to help those kids talk to Santa last Christmas!"*

"Partly," Kim said. "Time to do another watch—can you stick around until I'm done?"

"I'd better go back. We'll catch up when you get off work—actually, I'm wondering what you can see—look at that stuff."

"Yeah, I know." Kim said, shaking her head at the thick layer of fog and low clouds rolling into the valleys. "If this keeps up, I won't have any visibility at all pretty soon. But this fog is a real bonus for the woods. The 'flash' point goes down as the moisture content rises."

"Spoken like a true lookout," Marc said smiling. "I just hope it doesn't rain, but if it does, we've got a couple of tents

*See *Hostage in the Woods*.

if we need them. Enough to keep the equipment dry, anyway. The humans can all come over here with you..."

"How cozy," Kim laughed.

But it didn't rain—just got foggier and foggier. Mid afternoon, Kim pulled on a sweatshirt. There wasn't really much she could see, but she felt she should stay close to the forestry radio in case she was needed.

The afternoon moved slowly. Heather and Theresa came over once to visit. Kim was grateful when six o'clock arrived. She put the binoculars down and hurried over to the Field Day site where the smell of frying hamburgers greeted her.

Richard, who had been appointed official record keeper for the group, showed her the long list of contacts—mostly American and Canadian, but enough foreign stations to impress anyone.

The operators took turns—one at the transceiver and another writing down calls while the others ate dinner. Kim had just been handed a cup of steaming hot chocolate when Marc held up his hand to silence the chatter.

"Listen," he said. "It's a small plane and it sounds like the engine is missing. Wonder how they can see in this soup, anyway?"

A deathly silence fell over the group as they tried to see through the whiteness around them. Suddenly, there was a sound like a tree falling and the flash of a silver wing pierced the misty shroud momentarily. Then the horrible thud of an impact, invisible in the fog, but so close that the ground shook.

Chapter 8

Tragedy in the Fog

Saturday, June 25th
8 p.m.

For a few seconds, the group of Amateur Radio operators looked at each other in stricken horror. Then the many hours spent practicing emergency communications in mock disaster drills overrode their shock, and they began to act. Richard, the club president, turned to Kim.

"It was over there to the east—have any idea of the location?"

"Just a vague one—we're going to have to hurry—it's getting dark already," she yelled as she ran to the lookout. "Organize things here—I'll go report it to Dispatch."

While Kim was gone, Richard assigned Jeff, N6UUO, and one of his friends to monitor the radios in the camp. An amateur who had just gotten his license the week before, Mike, went up to be by the forestry radio in the lookout. The rest grabbed blankets and flashlights and joined Kim as she came racing back with a first-aid kit.

"Okay," she said breathlessly. "I called it in—they're sending emergency vehicles up here right now. Mike will relay any further information from them to us. Let's go see if we can find the plane."

They set off on the trail leading down the hill. Visibility was terrible, but they headed toward the area where they had seen the plane cut through the fog. At the bottom of the first hill, the trail turned west leading down to the valley.

"Over there," said Richard. "I'm sure it's over there." He pointed at the heavily wooded hillside across a ravine from them. They scrambled down the rocky embankment, sending stones flying. At one point, Kim sat down and scooted rather

than risk falling. Soon, they were all running up the other side through the thickly treed hillside.

"Listen," Marc said.

They paused. It was almost totally dark now, and the damp fog made them feel like ghosts wandering in limbo. Above the rustle of wind in the trees, there was the sound of creaking metal.

"I bet they're just over the top," Marc said.

They spread out and ran toward different points of the crest.

"Over here," Heather yelled.

She was pointing to the left at a small grove of trees set off from the main forest. A light Cessna aircraft was wedged vertically sideways, one wing tip touching the ground while the rest of the plane was held precariously suspended by the huge Douglas fir branches. Kim could hear the sound of a baby whimpering as they raced over to the crash.

"Careful!" Marc cautioned. "We don't want to jar the plane."

"Help!" a woman's voice cried pitifully.

"Don't move!" Richard yelled back to the voice in the creaking aircraft. "We'll get you out."

He aimed the beam of his flashlight toward the cockpit.

A man was slumped over the control panel in the pilot's seat. The woman who had cried out was moving around in the seat next to him.

"Hold still," Richard cautioned again.

Marc had already begun climbing the trunk of one of the trees. Hand over hand, he pulled himself up through the branches until he was level with the windows of the cockpit on the woman's side.

"I think I can get in there," he yelled down to the group, "but I'm afraid I'll knock the whole thing loose."

"We've got to get to them some way," Richard said as he motioned for the group to stand clear of where the plane might fall if Marc's added weight brought it down through the branches.

They watched anxiously as Marc leaned out from the tree and eased the plane's door open. With one foot on the doorway and one foot still braced against the tree trunk, he leaned inside the plane. They could hear him talking quietly to whoever was inside. In a few minutes, he shimmied back down the tree.

"I think the man's dead," he said to the group. "Unfortunately, we'll have to get him out before we can slide the woman down the wing. I can't tell how bad her injuries are—she's got some cuts, but she was talking to me okay. There's a baby strapped in a car seat in the back—looks okay, just scared."

The persistent shrill cry of the infant made them all look up at the unstable fuselage of the plane. Kim directed her flashlight up the wing that was touching the ground and which led vertically to the cockpit. A small trickle of gasoline was seeping from the single engine on the fuselage and running down the wing.

"We'd better hurry," she said grimly.

Richard hastily knotted one of the blankets at one end to form a sling.

"Here, I'll go," he said. "I'm a paramedic."

"No, let me go," Marc said, already climbing back up the tree. "I'm lighter!"

"See if she can move her hands and feet—if not, we'll have to rig a backboard," Richard told him as they watched Marc gingerly edge his way from the tree back into the tilting cockpit. Marc held onto the doorway with one hand and caught the knotted blanket Richard threw.

Now the lifeless form of the man was clearly visible in the beam of their lights. Kim could vaguely see Marc checking for a pulse and listening for breathing. The baby's cries grew more shrill. The woman was weeping.

"Hurry!" Kim breathed softly as the plane shook under the added weight. Marc unstrapped the man and tried to ease his body into the blanket sling.

"I can't lower him and still hang on here," Marc called down.

"Hang on," Richard said. "You may be lighter, but I'm coming up anyway."

Kim reached out and grabbed Heather's hand for reassurance as the plane quaked and creaked under the double weight of two men. Richard edged his body halfway up the wing.

"Okay," he said. "Give me his feet."

Marc half wedged himself into the doorway of the small aircraft and managed to lower the man's limp body onto the blanket on the wing. Still holding on to the top of the blanket, he slid the heavy sling into Richard's waiting grasp. Then it was just a matter of Richard sliding with the man down the wing tip into the outstretched hands of the waiting group.

Somberly, they watched as Richard quickly checked the man over. He stood and shook his head sadly.

"There's nothing we can do for him—I think he was dead on impact. From the appearance of his pupils, he must have taken quite a blow to his head."

Bob, W6AAQ, another ham with the group, had already climbed back up the wing with a second blanket sling to help Marc with the woman. It was reassuring to hear her voice—at least she was alive!

Carefully, she was lowered down the wing. The group carried her over to the clearing, a distance from her husband.

"My little girl," she cried. "Get my baby."

Theresa knelt beside her and held her hand.

"We are—they're bringing her out right now."

Richard quickly checked the woman over and talked to her quietly. She said her name was Sue Williams. She answered questions, but she was too distraught to talk much.

Other than a deep cut to her forehead and a possible broken left arm, she didn't seem to be seriously injured. Heather held a pressure bandage in place on the cut while Richard turned his attention to the baby who had stopped crying the minute Marc loosened her car seat. Because they didn't know if she was injured, Marc and Bob had decided it was safest to just lower the baby supported by the rigid back of the infant carrier.

Now on the ground, it was obvious she was fine. In fact, she smiled up at the concerned faces looking down at her and waved her arms. Richard examined her gently and then laid her on the blanket while he splinted her mother's arm. When her left arm was properly immobilized, Sue Williams reached out with her right hand to draw the baby close and kiss her.

I wonder why she doesn't ask about her husband, Kim thought. Then she saw her looking over in the direction of his still form near the airplane. *She knows,* she thought. Kim felt tears welling up in her own eyes.

Bob was talking on his two-meter rig to the hams back at the Field Day site, giving them directions to their location. He paused and turned to the group.

"The emergency vehicles are at the trailhead now—they're bringing stretchers up. It's going to be a good hour until they get here. It's too bad they weren't able to bring a helicopter up to the landing site by the lookout, but in this fog, it's unthinkable. Because there's a death, they're bringing a deputy medical examiner along too."

Bob and Heather had propped Sue Williams up against blankets. The baby seemed cold and was crying again. Theresa wrapped her in a blanket and handed her to Kim.

"Here, hold her while I go get something," Theresa said.

She ran to the edge of the clearing and came back with a thermos of hot tea she had grabbed as the group left their campsite.

"You really will make a good ham," Kim whispered to her. "You think of everything!"

Theresa poured a cup of tea for Sue Williams and helped her drink. Gradually, the distraught woman quieted and began to tell what had happened. Kim held the baby close to her body and stood rocking gently back and forth until her tiny eyes closed, and she nestled her head against Kim's shoulder.

The baby's mother watched her anxiously.

"Your daughter's fine," Kim reassured her. "See, she's sucking her thumb." She turned so the woman could see the baby's peaceful face.

"We left Eureka at noon," Sue began in a quavering voice. "John, that's my husband—he wanted to take us on a business trip with him. He's only had his pilot's license for six months—he's a really good pilot though. We stopped in Eugene for more fuel. The weather report said something about low fog, but he said we'd be way above it. I don't know what happened...I think we got a little lost and then all of a sudden, we were in the fog and something started going wrong with the engine and..." She began crying again.

Heather and Theresa both put their arms around her and sat on the ground holding her. The group was silent. Bill picked up a flashlight.

"Come on, Marc. Let's go back to camp and meet the rescue workers so we can lead them here."

Richard nodded at the two men.

"Go ahead—we're fine here. I'll leave this beacon light on so you can use it as a reference point."

Richard had made one more trip up the wing of the downed aircraft. He came back carrying a diaper bag and a small suitcase.

"Don't worry, we'll get all your things out," he told Sue.

She looked up and smiled wanly at him.

"There's a bottle of formula in the bag. When my daughter wakes up, she may be hungry."

Sure enough, as if on cue, the baby yawned and opened her eyes. When she began to whimper, Kim laid her down beside her mother.

"The milk's probably cold by now," Sue said.

Kim looked through the diaper bag until she found the bottle.

"Here," Theresa said, handing her a cup of steaming tea. "Set the bottle in this for a few minutes."

Kim did as Theresa suggested and while the bottle warmed, she picked up the baby and carried her, talking to her in a comforting voice. Heather and Bob made faces at her and were rewarded by a tiny laugh. Then Kim settled down on the blanket beside Sue, cradling the baby while she gave her the bottle. When the milk was half gone, she closed her eyes and fell asleep.

"They've reached the camp," Richard said, his two-meter rig held to his ear. "Marc and Bill are leading them over here now."

He handed his transceiver to Heather and made one last trip up the wing of the plane. He brought back a few more baby things.

"We need to leave everything else in the plane," Richard said. "The FAA inspectors will want to examine the crash site to try and determine a cause."

"I see them," said Theresa, standing on the top of the crest.

She waved her flashlight and shouted down to the approaching group. Bill and Marc led the four emergency workers in. One of them went to the plane and shut off the transmitter, a device which had been sending emergency signals since impact. Sue Williams was transferred to a stretcher while the medical examiner went over to check on the dead pilot. Another of the rescue workers came over to Kim who was holding the baby.

"She seems to be okay," Kim said. "Eating, sleeping—even laughed once for us."

Together, they strapped the baby back into the infant seat. She stirred slightly and smiled in her sleep, but she was oblivious to the activity around her. In a few minutes, they were off down the dark trail again. Theresa walked ahead carrying a lantern. Two rescue workers with assistance from Marc and Bill carried the injured woman on a stretcher. Kim and Heather took turns carrying the baby.

Richard and Bob remained behind with the sheriff's deputy and medical examiner to provide assistance. They would lead the workers back to camp when they completed their tasks.

"My husband," said Sue Williams softly as they rounded a corner in the darkness and headed back to camp.

"He'll be brought out later," one of the workers told her.

It was midnight before the group returned to the Field Day site. After a brief stop, Sue Williams was transported down the hill to a waiting ambulance. The rest of the group sat around talking quietly about the evening's events.

Someone made hot chocolate, and gratefully, the weary Amateur Radio operators accepted the offered cups. Surprisingly, there was little conversation.

The Field Day transceiver had been turned off. Everyone looked downcast as they reflected on the tragedy of the past hours. Bill reached over and turned the rig back on.

"CQ Field Day, CQ Field Day." It was a station in Maine calling—5 by 9—literally booming in.

"You know, we came up here to work some DX," said Marc. "There's nothing more we can do for that family so let's get back on the air."

There were some murmurs of agreement as a couple of people moved over to man the rig. Kim watched for awhile and then yawned.

"I'm afraid I've got to go to bed—tomorrow's another work day," Kim said.

There were hugs goodnight. The group had become more than just a bunch of people interested in the same hobby. Now, it seemed as if they were one big family. Kim trudged up the trail to the lookout. Waves of exhaustion swept over her, and she knew that in spite of the sadness she felt, she would sleep.

Chapter 9

Blue Skies, Green Plants, and Soft Jazz

Saturday, July 2nd
In the skies above the Cascades

"C an't believe this weather—first clear day we've had in a week," Detective Sarah Brinks said above the noise of the single engine plane.

"It's been pretty thick, all right," the pilot, Mel Jackson replied.

The two of them were returning from the season's first routine drug surveillance flight conducted by the sheriff's department. It would be much later in the season when their chances would increase of seeing flowering marijuana, but due to the growing drug problems in the U.S., it was imperative that law enforcement agencies be watchful every month of the year.

Detective Brinks, whose specialty was aerial surveillance, had gone through a program to learn how to be a spotter. Her keen eyesight aided by binoculars and a skilled pilot had been responsible for the confiscation of many drug patches before they could be sold to spread their lethal poison into society. She found it hard to describe the hue of the flashy green that flowering marijuana plants turned, but she said that once you had seen it, it was impossible to forget.

"The word is," she said to the pilot, "that this year the patches will be even smaller and farther apart—making it harder for us to spot."

Mel nodded in agreement.

"Well, we sure haven't seen anything today other than that elk herd—let's finish this area and then we'll head for home. I doubt we're going to see anything unless they're standing right out there stringing camouflage netting, but we'll keep looking," Sarah said.

The pilot banked the plane gently and swept along the southern exposure of the hillsides. Sarah focused her binoculars on the terrain below, paying close attention to anything that might appear to be out of the ordinary—netting, plastic pipes, dead fir needles from lower branches having been cut to allow more sunlight into growing areas.

"Go back over that slope there, would you?" she asked Mel.

He circled the plane around and brought it in a little lower. There was a young woman standing out on the deck of a fire lookout tower, and he waggled the wings in response to her wave.

"No, I guess not," Sarah said. "I thought for a moment, I saw some white pipes, but I don't see them now. We may want to recheck that area a few weeks down the road."

Mel resumed his course toward the Salem airport, and Sarah put her binoculars back in their case.

* * * * * * * *

Far below the circling aircraft, 3,000 young marijuana plants were participating in the natural phenomenon of photosynthesis.* With water, soil, and sunlight to provide nourishment, they were growing rapidly. And yes, as one of the botanical inhabitants of the earth, they were producing oxygen as a by-product. But their growers weren't interested in improving the earth's atmosphere; they were interested in the narcotic content of the plants. It was a by-product which could make them rich.

* * * * * * * *

---

*Photosynthesis: the process by which green plants manufacture a simple sugar from carbon dioxide and water in the presence of light and chlorophyll, with oxygen produced as a by-product.

Saturday, July 9th
Vista Peak and Portland

Kim woke up and looked out the window. Fog again! Not only fog, but it was drizzling. She had always liked cool, misty weather before—now it brought to mind the sad circumstances of the plane crash which had killed Mr. Williams. She sighed, remembering the past two weeks.

It had been a fairly quiet time for Kim—she welcomed the solitude after the events of Field Day. She had been up and down the hill several times—on foggy days, the Detroit Ranger Station liked her to come down and help with paperwork. She had even managed a quick trip home for one night, grateful for the chance to do her much needed laundry. The fog cleared the next day, so Kim went back up to the lookout.

It was sunny and hot through the 4th, a particularly vulnerable time for the forests when they faced destruction from man's carelessness with both campfires and fireworks. But this year, all of the publicity must have worked. Kim spent the entire Fourth of July without spotting a single smoke. In the evening, she sat on the deck and watched glimmers of fireworks from the skies above cities in the Willamette Valley.

Then as if Mother Nature had spent her store of sunshine on the national holiday, the fog rolled back in, this time with an accompanying light drizzle. For the first time since the first of June, the forest fire danger was rated "high" instead of "extreme."

The Dispatch Center supervisor had called Kim Friday night suggesting she take Saturday off if the same marine weather pattern continued. Now she peered out her window at the blanketing white. The tree tops looked like ghostly sentinels in the shroud of fog. Quickly, she called into headquarters to double check that her day off was still okay.

With her two-meter radio, she called Marc to tell him the "date" was on. She had talked to her parents the night before with a "phone patch," and they had agreed to drive up to the trailhead at 6:30 a.m. If Kim didn't show up by 7:30, they would know her plans had changed and would hike up to see her instead.

Hastily she dressed and went out on the deck. The fog was so thick there was nothing to scan. She locked the lookout, slipped the key in her pocket, and set off down the hill. The welcome sight of her parents' car greeted her as she came around the last curve in the trail. Her father was sitting with the car door open, reading the paper while her mother walked around in the small clearing.

"Hi, Honey," Mrs. Stafford greeted her with a kiss on the cheek. "Have you had breakfast?"

"No, not yet, and I'm starved!"

Her father smiled. "You always were a good eater," he teased. Until Kim's first year of college, when she had put on a few pounds, her ability to eat enormous amounts without gaining an ounce had always amazed her family.

"Actually, Dad, I'll have you know, I think I've lost about ten pounds. All my clothes are too big," Kim replied.

"You look great—how do you do it?" her mother said.

"Want to come be a lookout with me, Mom? I guarantee you it's the perfect weight loss and exercise program."

"No thanks, Kim. I think I'll just stay the way I am," her mother laughed.

They stopped at a small cafe, and Mr. and Mrs. Stafford had toast and coffee while Kim devoured a cheese and spinach omelette and a stack of hot cakes. Kim's mother had brought along a pink flowered sundress for her and Kim went to the restroom to change from her shorts and hiking boots to more feminine attire.

"I'm glad you brought along the sweater," Kim said as she came back to the table. "I can't believe how cold it's gotten."

"Well, enjoy it while it lasts," her father said. "The long term forecast is for it to start heating up—really heating up tomorrow."

The Staffords got in the car and drove on to Portland. Kim's parents wanted to do some shopping plus visit an aunt who lived in Beaverton while Kim spent the afternoon with Marc. He had managed to get the day off from his construction work. When they drove up to the Lawrences' house, Marc was standing in the front yard. Even though he and Kim had been in constant contact on the radio for the past twenty miles, they greeted each other as though they had been apart for months. The Lawrences invited them in and they visited for half an hour.

"Oh, I almost forgot—I have something to show you," Marc said, reaching for the large manila envelope on the table. "Richard, KA7OZO, brought it over last night."

"What's this?" Kim asked staring at the embossed certificate inside.

"Well, as you know, we didn't stand a chance of winning any of the Field Day contest categories—not after we were off the air for half the night. But Richard wrote up what happened and sent it in with our contest forms. This is a special commendation certificate from the American Radio Relay League for service to our fellow man."

"It's nice," said Kim admiring the calligraphy on the certificate. "But it makes me sad—I just wish Mr. Williams had lived too."

I know," said Marc. "I guess we should be grateful that his wife and child survived. They're just lucky they landed in the trees."

"And now," he said, changing the subject on purpose, "if we're going to get to the Saturday Market with any time to look around before the jazz program, we had better get going."

Kim agreed to meet her parents back at the Lawrences at 5 o'clock. That way, they could drive her back to the lookout trail, and she could hike back up before dark.

"Do you miss your Chevy?" Kim asked as she climbed into Marc's four wheel drive pickup.

"Well, sort of—it was like an old friend. I've only had this a month so I'm not quite used to it, but it sure has a lot more room for my music instruments. And, the four wheel drive should come in handy next winter."

"I see you had your license plates transferred over," Kim said admiring the KA7ITR plates on the truck.

"You bet—first thing I did."

They got in the truck and drove west toward the Saturday Market, a weekly open-air market of arts and foods held under Portland's famous Burnside Bridge. Marc smiled as he watched Kim staring out the window at the sights of Portland.

"Gee, I've never seen you look so intent before—you're like a person who's been in isolation for 10 years and is just now seeing the world."

"In a way, that's true," Kim laughed. "I've gotten so used to the mountain quiet that I feel like all my senses are being assailed. I had forgotten what exhaust smells like."

"Ah, the perfume of the city," said Marc taking a deep breath. "Just wait until we get to the market—you won't believe all the stuff you'll smell cooking."

"I just ate, but give me another hour, and I'll be ready for it," Kim laughed, patting her stomach.

"That's what I like," Marc said—"a woman who eats. I can't imagine dating someone who just nibbles at dainty little watercress sandwiches."

They continued their friendly teasing banter while Marc found a place to park the truck. Then they walked, hand in hand, to the market place. A man dressed in blue denim overalls with a red bandana tied around his forehead played the accordion on a street corner.

On the opposite corner, artists sat in front of their booths, selling everything from tie-dyed t-shirts to environmentally safe soap. Kim and Marc made their way up and down the line of merchants, admiring the hand-made products and chatting with their designers. Kim bought a small bag of strawberry tea and a little wooden dog with moveable legs and tail.

"Christmas present for my cousin," she explained.

"I guess we'd better get something to eat before the concert," Marc said. "Starts in an hour, and I'd like to stake out a good place on the grass."

Kim decided on stir-fried vegetables served upright in a whole wheat tortilla like an ice cream cone. Marc chose a spicy Korean dish of beef and cabbage. They ate their food while walking through the market area and then crossed the street to the shady park bordering the Willamette River.

"I know," Kim said as Marc steered them to a vacant spot of grass to the right of the stage. "You want to sit where you have a good view of the bass player."

"How did you ever guess?" Marc asked teasing.

The performance started promptly at one, and for the next two hours, Kim and Marc sat and listened to a mixture of fusion and soft jazz. An occasional boat passed under the bridge, and seagulls circled and swooped over the river.

Kim closed her eyes in the warm sun and let the music fill her head. She couldn't remember when she'd felt happier. Whenever she looked at Marc, his eyes were intently focused on the man playing the five string fretless bass. She watched the half smile on Marc's face—it was a good feeling to be with someone who was enjoying something so much.

All too soon, the afternoon was over. Kim and Marc picked up their belongings and hurried back to his truck.

"I wish," Marc said, as they pulled into his driveway, "that we could spend a lot more afternoons like that."

"Me too," Kim said softly.

Just then, Kim's parents drove up. Marc reached out and took Kim's hand.

"I guess this is it until I see you again—when will that be?"

"Can you come up for my birthday next month—Saturday the 20th?"

"That's right before I go to Sunriver—I'll be there," Marc promised. He kissed her gently on the cheek, and they got out of the truck.

* * * * * * *

"It's all of a sudden gotten real hot," said Kim's mother, fanning herself as they turned off Interstate 5 to Highway 20 leading up into the Cascades.

"Yes, I know," said Kim sounding worried. "I hope they haven't sent someone else up to my lookout because the weather changed."

"What would be the big deal if they did?" her father asked.

"Oh, I don't know," Kim shrugged. "I guess I just feel kind of a possession of that area—it's my job to take care of it."

"You're going to make a good mother," Mrs. Stafford laughed.

"Okay," Kim laughed. "Just get me back to my family of little trees."

They drove along the fir-lined highway past Detroit Lake and the Ranger Station. Soon, they had reached the trail head. Kim had changed back into her hiking clothes at Marc's house before leaving, and she handed her folded sundress back to her mother.

"Thanks you two for making it a perfect day."

Kim's parents hugged her good-bye, and Kim set off up the trail, carrying a backpack of goodies from her parents.

"You be careful!" her mother called out after her.

"I will," Kim promised.

Chapter 10

"Hotter than..."

Tuesday, July 12th
Vista Peak Lookout

"Hotter than a firecracker," Kim used to say when she was little. Her grandfather had more colorful comparisons. But no matter what the words, it was hot. Kim sighed and wrapped a bandana soaked in cool water around her neck as she went out onto the blazing deck to do her quarter-hour scan.

Mother Nature could certainly reverse herself in a hurry. Replacing the cool fog of the week before were two days of record-breaking temperatures. Kim had heard from one of the other lookouts that Salem had toasted under 104 degree weather Monday, and the forecast was for 106 today. It was perhaps ten degrees cooler in the mountains, but still it seemed unbearably hot.

The solid window walls heated up the lookout like a bake oven. Kim had spent last night sleeping on the deck. The mosquitoes had shared her campsite, and now she scratched at several welts on her face and arms.

All she felt like doing was lying down in cool water. She thought wistfully of the cold stream fifteen minutes away. Maybe tonight there would be time to get some buckets of ice cold water. She was beginning to doubt if she would get away from the lookout at all today. The smokes had been almost continuous. There was another one now—off to the west of her. She ran inside to get an azimuth and heard Alyse's calm voice call it in before she had a chance to reach her microphone. Quickly, Kim called in a cross shot. Alyse had told her that fire units started to move after the first call, but backups or cross shots were helpful in confirming the location.

Alyse came back on the radio briefly and asked Kim to get on two-meter simplex.

"KA7SJP from N7NYJ. Are you as hot as we are, Kim?"

"Hotter," Kim laughed.

"Let's hope this doesn't last too long, but from what I hear, it's supposed to be hot the rest of the month."

"Great," Kim groaned.

"Have you rigged yourself a shade to sit under?" Alyse asked.

"Sort of," Kim said. "There was a partial canopy attached to one side of the lookout, and I've tried to extend it a bit with a canvas tarp I had. Trouble is that doesn't help when I'm walking the perimeter trying to see things. And inside the lookout is just unbearable. I slept outside last night."

"Hang in there, Kim. Make sure you wear a hat—sunstroke is no joke. And it helps to take a few ice cubes and wrap them in something to put on the back of your neck."

"I've already tried that, but I think I like eating them the best. Oops, there's another smoke—gotta go."

This time Kim beat Alyse to the call and the Sisi lookout gave his cross shot.

By late afternoon, the temperature was 96 at the lookout. Kim watched a blue jay forage for food in the dry soil. He stopped and regarded Kim, his beak open in the dry breathless air. A breeze rustled through the dead leaves and fir needles on the ground, as he fluttered up to a low branch. Kim turned her eyes skyward.

The wind was picking up and directly to the west she could see a huge bank of dense thunderclouds.

"Cumulonimbus," she said aloud to herself. "I wonder if we're going to get wet?"

The weather report this morning had warned of the possibility of thunder showers, but up until now, the clear hot skies seemed to be refuting that forecast.

Suddenly, there was a zig zag of lightning in the distance. and then ten seconds later, the distinctive clap of thunder. Kim watched in fascination as the electrically charged clouds approached. Zap! Another flash—this time cloud to ground. Automatically, Kim began to count aloud.

"One thousand one, one thousand two, one thousand three, one thousand four..."

Boom! The roll of thunder made her jump. She had learned years ago that since light travels at 186,000 miles a second and sound at 1,100 feet a second, that by counting the seconds between the flash of lightning and the thunder and then dividing by five would give an approximate distance in miles of the strike. Another flash—this time cloud to cloud. As she counted, she imagined the huge amount of electrical energy contained within the storm cloud. More energy than a hydrogen bomb.

"One, one thousand...two..." Boom!

The storm was moving with incredible speed over the mountains. There had been several lightning strikes to the ground and as the valley behind the storm began to clear, Kim could see several smokes in the distance.

Quickly, she moved inside and sat on her wooden stool well away from the metal stack of her woodstove. The lookout's lightning rod should attract and ground out any hits and unless the percussion of one shattered the windows, she should be safe in the all wood and glass structure. She thought she heard other lookouts calling in smokes, but the static electricity in the radio area was causing so much crackling noise, she couldn't really hear. As she had been instructed to do when a storm moved within a mile, Kim disconnected the radio and used the jackset as a hand-held.

The booms, claps, and crashes moved directly overheard and Kim instinctively crouched down on her stool. Then, just as suddenly as the storm had moved over her, it was off to the east and once again, she could count an interval between the flashes and the thunder. The rain was pelting the lookout. Cautiously, she moved to the west window and surveyed the valley, marking lightning strikes on her map as she saw them hit. Less than a mile from her, she could see several plumes of smoke.

Apparently, there had been so many smoke reports that the Willamette Dispatch in Eugene had turned radio communication over to each of the Ranger districts. Kim and the other district lookouts called in spotted fires directly to the Detroit Ranger Station.

The rain, although heavy, had been very brief, and several of the lightning strikes flared into substantial fires. Kim watched the closest one, about a half mile from her, as it fueled itself from the bone dry timber and plentiful oxygen. There was very little distance between two of the blazes, and like wild demons, they merged together with fiery intensity.

Kim moved out on the catwalk, surprised to find the water from the brief rain already evaporated. The fire was generating its own hot winds, and blistering air laced with ash struck her in the face. The smoke from this blaze was really obscuring her vision to the west. Quickly, she scanned to the north, south, and east to make sure there weren't any new smokes behind her.

"Vista Peak from Detroit."

Kim grabbed the forestry microphone.

"Vista Peak—go ahead."

"What's your situation up there, Kim?"

"The fire is out of control and is moving rapidly in my direction," Kim said, trying to keep the nervousness out of her voice.

"Kim, we want you to evacuate now. Someone will pick you up at the trailhead in 30 minutes. Move quickly."

"Copy, Detroit."

Kim grabbed a few of her belongings to stuff into a backpack—a photo of Marc, her diary, a canteen and bandana, her two-meter rig. "Jessie!" For a second, she considered disconnecting it, but she knew its weight would slow her down. Transceivers could be replaced. Human life couldn't.

She closed the lookout door behind her, saying a quick prayer as she ran down the steps. The searing wind made her skin prickle as she ran down the trail. There was a tanker plane overhead. She heard the lumbering roar of the DC7 as it flew directly overhead. The sound of tall timber exploding with fire joined the din in her ears. Panting heavily from the heat, she wrapped her water soaked kerchief over her nose and mouth and raced down the hill.

* * * * * * * *

Sil Myers was a legend at the Redmond Air Tanker Base. Legend for his military record in Vietnam and in recent years for his strike accuracy flying the huge C130s and DC7s carrying their fire retardant load of reddish brown "slurry," an ammonium phosphate compound. The slurry was dropped in "doors" meaning a partial drop or in "salvos," everything at once, often right at the head of a fire. Sil liked salvos the best.

Most people thought it was hard to tell what Sil liked. Although he whistled a lot, his general attitude toward life seemed pessimistic. The staff often joked about his favorite expression "Don't worry about anything because nothing will ever be all right."

"Just what does that mean?" his copilot, Lance Rettig, KB7NLD, had asked him once.

"Look at the world," Sil had replied.

Lance hadn't asked him again. Now the two of them were flying through the turbulent hot air created by the fire. Sil stopped whistling, as Dispatch radioed in exact coordinates of the drop they should make.

"Bingo," he said softly as the C130 plane released 2000 pounds of reddish-brown oozy compound. He banked the plane and flew around to observe his drop. The fire seemed to be momentarily halted in its eastward path. Another tanker, a DC7 was close on his tail to hit another flank of the fire.

"Do you think that's going to be 'all right?'" Lance joked with him.

"Don't know—guess we'll have to read the papers tomorrow," Sil said.

* * * * * * * *

Kim waited out the fire at the Ranger Station. After a quick call to her parents to assure them she was okay, she showered at the bunkhouse and then sat glued to the radios, listening to the talk between the various fire and forest agencies. As darkness fell, no one could tell her if her lookout had been spared.

She slept fitfully on a spare bunk in the bunkroom. Sne considered getting up several times in the night to go into the station and listen to the radio but convinced herself that there was nothing she could do about the situation anyway. At daybreak, she was up and listening anxiously to the radio. The fire had been contained! She asked permission to talk to Coffin Mountain briefly and told Alyse to meet her on two meters.

"It's okay," Alyse said. "I can see your lookout station and it looks like the fire stopped about 1000 yards from the base."

Kim felt tears of relief come to her eyes as she thanked Alyse.

"When can I get back up there?" she asked one of the rangers. "I want to get back up there as soon as I can."

* * * * * * * *

Thursday, July 14th
10 a.m.

Kim coughed at the smoke wafting upward from the charred ground. Breathing was so difficult that she found it hard to walk very fast up the trail to the lookout. Just as Alyse had said, the fire had been stopped miraculously short of the west side of the lookout.

Mop up crews of fire fighters were still in the area, extinguishing suspicious timbers and making sure that no spark remained. After looking at their weary, soot-streaked faces, Kim didn't notice her own discomfort anymore. She couldn't even imagine what it would be like to be at the front line of such an inferno.

There it was! Vista Peak Lookout completely intact. She paused at the curve in the trail and admired the glass building. Never had home looked so inviting. Kim ran the last few yards and raced up the stairs.

The windows on the west side of the building were streaked with a reddish-brown residue. Kim put her finger to the compound and smelled it. Then she realized it was some of the chemicals dropped by the tankers. The hillside directly below her was also coated with the stuff. She ran her hand along the railing with its paint blistered from the intense heat. How close they had come to losing this lookout!

With a rush of emotion, she went inside and looked around. Everything was just as she had left it. She certainly wouldn't have begrudged the fire fighters drinking her water, but it didn't appear that anyone had come in. She grabbed a rag and a bottle of window cleaner and went out to tackle the red-streaked windows. By noon, the glass was sparkling again, and Kim reported proudly to Dispatch that she was back in service.

The thunderstorm was long gone, and once again the forest valleys baked under hot sunshine. Kim put on her coolest shorts and a tank top and padded barefoot back and forth on the deck.

Amazingly after such a maelstrom, there were no new fires today. The afternoon wore on. Kim had a brief QSO with Marc at dinner time. She stayed on duty until 8 and then slipped down to the creek for that cool shower she had been dreaming of yesterday. As she was getting dressed, her eye caught some silver forms drifting down the stream. More dead fish. How strange, Kim thought, as she picked one up and turned it over in her hands. She would have to mention that to Jack the next time he came up.

* * * * * * * *

"I'm sorry sir, we aren't letting anyone into this area until the fire crews are all done," the Forest Service personnel said to Jay at a checkpoint on Highway 22. He glanced briefly at Jay's firewood permit and added, "The fire danger's way too high to allow cutting even if there weren't a fire."

Jay put the permit back in his pocket and sighed. He backed up the truck and turned around.

"Whatcha gonna do now?" Lenny asked curiously.

Jay drove 100 yards down the road and then pulled over to the side.

"Hand me the BLM map in the glove compartment," he ordered Lenny. "See," he said, pointing to a faint line on the map near the location. "There's another road near the backside of our field. It will be a hike and probably some fence climbing, but we've got to find out what happened."

Jay drove the truck down the bumpy road until they came to a gate. The gates had been redesigned in the last few years with more secure locking devices to prevent incursions by unwanted people such as Jay and Lenny. It would take dynamite to blow the lock off this gate. Jay sighed and parked the truck under the shade of an alder tree.

"Let's get moving," he said to Lenny.

Lenny groaned. He groaned again much louder two hours later after what seemed like an interminable jungle hike. But Jay had been right. There was another way to their growing field. And when they got there, they found the plants intact. Brutus seemed calm—just hungry and thirsty as usual. More important, the fire had been far enough away that it was unlikely fire crews would come tromping through their field. That was very good news.

Chapter 11

The Circus Comes to Town

Friday, July 15th
Vista Peak Lookout 5 a.m.

Kim turned over in her bunk and pulled the sleeping bag over her shoulders, dreaming she was on a fishing boat with her father. It was swaying in the ocean swells, back and forth, back and forth. Something wasn't right in the dream, though. Fighting through the depths of sleep, she forced herself to wake up. She opened her eyes and sat bolt upright in bed. The whole lookout was swaying!

Earthquake? No, she had been in a California earthquake, and this didn't have the rumbling tremor of an earthquake. It was more like the gentle swaying of a hammock in the breeze. In the fierce winds of the fire earlier in the week, the lookout had been rock steady. Kim looked out the windows in the early morning light. The trees were quiet. The swaying stopped, and then suddenly, a screeching bellow filled the air. Kim's eyes opened wide in terror. What on earth?

Cautiously, she tiptoed out on the deck, looked over, and then jumped back. Two beady eyes stared back at her. Eyes connected to the largest elephant Kim had ever seen in her life. Gasping, she rubbed her own eyes. *I must be seeing things*, she thought. But then the elephant put its trunk against the corner of the deck and shoved gently. Kim felt the platform sway under her. She definitely wasn't dreaming!

"Hi," she said to the huge creature and then laughed at herself.

To her surprise, the elephant looked back, in what Kim hoped was a friendly manner, and extended the tip of its trunk toward her bare toes.

"Just a minute," Kim said.

She ran inside and grabbed a handful of peanuts and laid them out along the edge of the platform. One by one, the elephant curled its trunk delicately around each nut and lowered it to its mouth.

By habit, Kim grabbed the binoculars and did a quick scan of the area. All was quiet. She grabbed the microphone to the forestry radio.

"Uh, Willamette Dispatch, uh, this is Vista Peak."

"Go ahead, Kim, what's up?"

"I'm not sure you're going to believe this, but, uh, I've got an elephant at my lookout."

She waited to hear laughter and perhaps the message that the little men in white coats were on their way to retrieve her. But instead Dispatch came right back to her.

"Oh good, that's where she is! A circus truck on its way to Bend went off Highway 22 last night near Detroit and several animals escaped. All except one elephant and two monkeys have been recaptured. By the way, her name is Samantha, and she's friendly."

"Samantha, huh? Well she seems nice enough, but I think maybe she thinks she's supposed to knock down the lookout."

There was a pause before Ralph, the dispatcher on duty, came back to her.

"Stand by a minute, Kim. I'm going to try to reach the driver."

Kim spread the last of her bag of peanuts out on the deck and thought frantically of any other treats she might have to offer this behemoth. Samantha consumed each of the peanuts and then reached her trunk questioningly along the deck, feeling each board. Kim patted her trunk gently.

"Vista Peak from Willamette Dispatch."

"This is Vista Peak."

"Kim, I talked to the circus driver. He's going to come up there as soon as he catches the monkeys. A couple of our people will join him to help. Right now, they're climbing trees after monkeys."

Kim couldn't help hear the suppressed laughter in Ralph's voice. But then he cleared his throat and continued.

"In the meantime, Kim, he says to try and keep Samantha in the area. He's afraid she may get hurt if she wanders off alone."

"Great, Ralph, and just how am I supposed to keep her?"

"I don't know, Kim. He didn't say, and I can't get hold of him now. Crew 42's radio isn't answering—I think they've got their hands full."

Just then, Samantha bellowed.

"Wow," Ralph said. "I think we could hear that even without the radio. Kim, you be careful—don't get too close to her."

"Copy," Kim said. "I gotta go. Vista Peak clear."

Samantha had become bored with Kim's inattention and was now meandering toward the trail leading to the outhouse.

"Oh, no," Kim whispered. She ran down the steps after the elephant.

"Here, Samantha, come here girl!" she yelled.

Samantha seemed intrigued with the small wooden structure that served as Kim's bathroom. She circled her trunk around it and then pushed her head up against one side of the building.

"No! Samantha, No!" Kim screeched.

The outhouse rocked back and forth on its support and then toppled over as easily as a sapling bending in the wind.

A few of the boards splintered, and the door that Kim had painted flowers on hung askew from one hinge.

"Oh, Samantha, how could you?" Kim cried.

The elephant turned at her voice and took a few steps toward her.

"Nice elephant, nice girl," Kim coaxed. "Your owner says you're a nice elephant. Let's hope that's true."

Scared, Kim stood perfectly still. The lumbering beast walked up to her and stopped beside her. Tentatively, Kim reached out and patted her trunk. The elephant made a soft grunting noise, and Kim stood on her tiptoes and scratched behind the elephant's huge ear. She seemed to remember seeing someone doing that in a movie.

Apparently, Samantha liked it okay too because she stood quietly. Then she began rooting around the ground with her trunk. A small patch of blue wildflowers that Kim had been encouraging with some of her precious water fell prey to Samantha's curiosity. She pulled the whole bunch up and chewed them carefully.

"So much for beautifying my surroundings," Kim groaned.

The elephant continued its search along the dusty ground.

"Why, I bet you're thirsty," Kim said. "You poor thing. Wait here a minute."

She thought of her own water supply and realized it would be just a sip for this huge animal. She checked in with Dispatch and told them the problem. She was going to try to lead Samantha down to the stream. When they got hold of the driver, they should tell him and the other crew members to turn left at the bottom of the hill leading to the lookout and to meet her at the waterfall on the stream. She hoped one of them was familiar with the area.

Grabbing her two-meter radio and slipping it into the deep pocket of her khaki shorts, she joined Samantha on the trail. Or rather, she followed Samantha on the trail. Samantha had raised her trunk, sniffed the wind, given another huge bellow, and was now moving at a fast elephant walk in the direction of the stream.

"I guess you know how to take care of your needs, don't you?" Kim said following the huge animal down the narrow trail.

Samantha veered from the trail and took a beeline through the heavy brush toward the stream.

"I don't have as thick a hide as you do, old girl," Kim said. "How about if I meet you there?"

The elephant's huge hindquarters were already disappearing through the dense brush. Kim trotted down the trail and took the path she had discovered earlier—not as good as the main trail, but at least she didn't have to forge her way through thickets.

Another gigantic bellow and then the sound of gallons of water splashing greeted Kim as she scrambled down the rocks to the stream. Samantha had discovered her waterfall bathing area, and she was making good use of it. Standing knee deep in the icy water, she was sucking up trunkful after trunkful of the mountain water and spraying it over her hot dusty shoulders. Kim laughed and perched on the rock outcropping at the top of the waterfall to watch.

Suddenly, a blast of cold water struck her full in the face.

"What!" Kim sputtered.

Samantha turned her back and resumed her bathing activities.

"What did you do that for? You think that's funny?" Then Kim was laughing. "You're right, it is pretty funny."

Samantha turned her head slightly toward Kim's voice but made no other recognition of her. She kneeled her huge body down in the stream so that the water lapped along her belly.

"I bet that feels good," Kim said, wiping the water from her own face.

"Kim! Kim!"

"Down here," Kim yelled to the approaching group.

She walked back up the slope to the trail to wave to the two crew members and the circus driver. He was a small man dressed in flowered pants, an oversized khaki shirt, and a soiled white French beret. He grasped a bamboo cane firmly in his left hand.

"Ah, Kim," he said half bowing graciously and taking her hand. "My name is Henri. I see Samantha has given you a bath. I should have warned you—she loves to include others in her water festivities."

"It's okay," Kim said laughing. "Actually, it feels good today. She's discovered a good place to cool off."

Henri scrambled down the rocky approach to the creek and began speaking to Samantha in rapid French. Kim understood a word now and then. Samantha seemed to get the message that she was supposed to leave this watery haven and go back down the hill to be cooped up in a truck again. She bellowed and scooped an enormous trunk of water.

"Watch out!" Henri yelled.

It was too late. Samantha showered the four of them with an icy rain.

"Oh, you naughty girl," Henri scolded in English. "Come on now—time to go home."

Reluctantly, Samantha put her head down and lumbered out of the stream toward Henri. Henri put his cane up behind Samantha's right ear and tugged gently.

"Come on along, dear," he said.

Like a meek child, she followed him up the trail, turning just once to look back wistfully at the water.

"She turned over my outhouse," Kim said.

"Oh, Samantha, you bad, bad girl. Let's go fix the damage you've done. I just hope it can be fixed."

"Oh, I'm sure it can," said Kim. "Don't scold her. She's really a very nice elephant."

Henri beamed with the compliment.

"Would you like to ride her?"

"Why, I uh, sure..." Kim stammered.

Henri gave Samantha a quick command, and she kneeled obediently for Kim to climb on her neck.

"Whoa..." Kim squealed as the big animal stood back up, and Kim swayed precariously back and forth. She reached forward and grabbed a handful of Samantha's loose skin for support. Slowly, they made their way back up to the lookout.

Kim turned to Tom Mentor, one of the foresters.

"Could you go inside the lookout and grab my camera? No one will believe me if I don't have a photo."

He obliged and for several minutes, Kim and Samantha and Henri posed for candid shots. Then Kim slid off her charge's neck to the platform of the lookout.

"Now my dear," Henri said to Kim. "Show me the damage my darling has done."

Kim pointed across the clearing at her overturned outhouse. Henri led Samantha over to the fallen structure and peered down into the lime pit below.

"If we put it back on top, it will be okay?" he questioned.

"Yes," Kim said, "but we need to get my antenna back up too."

Henri spoke rapidly in French to Samantha who shoved her trunk underneath one side of the structure. With a seemingly effortless heave, she lifted it back upright and with the help of the three men, it was replaced properly. Kim secured the antenna. Henri looked sadly at the door broken from one of its hinges.

"Don't worry about that," Kim said. "I've got tools inside and I can fix it."

"Samantha, tell the beautiful young lady, you are sorry for all the trouble you caused her."

The elephant put her trunk out solemnly and Kim patted it and then the huge cheek.

"Good-bye, Samantha. You can come visit anytime you want, and we'll go bathing together."

The men all laughed and then they turned to take Samantha back down the trail. Kim waved good-bye and returned to the lookout.

"Willamette Dispatch from Vista Peak."

"Go ahead, Kim."

"The elephant has been captured and I'm back on duty."

"Any casualties?" Ralph laughed.

"Just my outhouse, but it'll live."

Kim imagined the ears of the Willamette Valley listening to this exchange and wondering what had transpired. What tales she would have to tell.

Just then Iron Mountain reported in with a smoke report.

Kim jumped. It was time to get back to work.

Chapter 12

Liquid Gold

Saturday, July 16th

"Whatcha buying all those pictures for?" Lenny complained as Jay scooped up half a dozen black and white prints of forest scenes at a Saturday flea market in Salem.

"You and me—we're photographers now," Jay said.

"Huh?" Lenny asked, his mouth hanging open.

"Look, stupid. With this heat, we've got to go up and water every day. The drip's just not doing the job with the stream down so far. There's only so many times people are going to believe we're cutting firewood. Probably, nobody is ever going to question us, but if they do, we're nature photographers."

Lenny just stared at him. Jay paid for his purchases and steered him toward the truck. They drove to a nearby shopping mall. Lenny stayed in the cab reading comic books while Jay went in to go shopping. When he emerged almost an hour later, his arms were laden with bulging parcels. He got into the truck and showed them quickly to Lenny.

"A 35mm Nikon, all sorts of lenses, tripod—the works."

"How long is it going to take you to learn to use all that stuff?" Lenny asked.

"Doesn't matter if I ever take a photo. We just have to look like we are. If anybody asks, we're working on a display for National Geographic—got it?"

"Yeah, sure," Lenny grumbled. "And supposin' we run into some other photographer in the woods who starts asking us questions about exposure, F stops and stuff?"

"Hey, that's good, Lenny. Where'd you learn all those fancy terms?"

"I used to work in the photo lab in junior high."

"Well, great, this will be a natural for you then," Jay said, reaching out to clap Lenny on the shoulder.

Lenny was silent until they were almost home.

"When do you think we can start harvesting?" he asked.

"If we can keep the water going, this heat will really increase their growth. Maybe, we can pull some in late August, if we're lucky."

"Fifty-fifty, right?" Lenny asked.

"That's what I said, partner. That's what it is."

* * * * * * * *

Saturday Afternoon
Vista Peak

Kim heard Bart's joyful barks long before she saw Jack and the mule train come around the crest of the hill. She did a quick scan of the valley and then ran down the steps to greet them. Although he had made only a couple of trips to see her, Bart greeted her like an old friend.

Kim laughed as he pranced back and forth, wagging his tail, and nuzzling her.

"Why hi, boy. Bet you're hot."

"Yeah, I almost didn't bring him," Jack said.

"Here let me get some water," Kim offered.

"No, he has his own canteen," Jack said, unstraping a canvas-covered water container from his horse. "Watch this."

He uncorked the bottle and poured a stream of water. Bart opened his mouth and caught the falling water mid air.

"Boy, Bart, you ought to be a circus dog."

Then in a rush, she told Jack about Samantha and all of her adventures in the thunderstorm the week before.

"Yeah, I heard that storm. Had ol' Bart here cringing under the bed. I called the station and offered to come get you on horseback, but they said you were already on your way down. I've been in a lot of thunderstorms in my life, and I still don't like them. Bart sure doesn't either."

Hearing his name, Bart barked happily in agreement.

"Oh, you are the silliest dog," Kim laughed, ruffling his ears and scratching him under the neck. "Come on you two, come on in and visit a little while. This has been a pretty quiet fire day."

After they had unloaded and stowed Kim's provisions, Jack moved the mules over to the shade at the edge of the clearing and tied them.

"I see you used most of your water this time," he said.

"Yeah, and I've been taking most of my water for bathing from the stream," Kim said. "It just seems like I drink a lot more in this heat. I've come to regard my supply as liquid gold!"

"It sure is, but, if you run out, you let me know, and we'll see about getting you some more."

Jack stayed for about an hour, talking to Kim in between her lookout duties. He and Bart gratefully accepted some ice cubes. Jack put his in a glass of ice tea Kim gave him, and Bart chewed his happily out on the deck.

"What are you working?" Jack asked her, nodding toward her transceiver.

"Just look at the log," Kim said.

"Whew, girl, is there any place you haven't worked in the last month?"

"Well, there wouldn't be if I had enough battery power. When I turn it off every night, I find it hard to go to sleep."

"Oh, that reminds me," Jack said, getting up. "I've got your mail out in the saddlebag. "There's a whole bunch of QSL cards in it."

He brought the bundle back in and together they spread the colorful cards out on the counter. It was fun to read the messages from the stations that she had worked. A young woman in Ecuador wrote, "God Bless you and your family." From South Africa, "I hope to travel to the U.S. soon—perhaps we can meet." "If you come to Australia, my home is your home while you are here," a ham wrote from Sidney.

"What are you going to do with all of these?" Jack asked.

"Put them on the bulletin board at home—wouldn't it be fun to meet each and every one of these people in person?" Kim commented.

"You know, you're young enough, you just might do that," Jack said. "Over the years, I've visited several of the hams I talked to during the summers I was a lookout."

They talked awhile more, and then reluctantly, Jack called to Bart and untied the mules.

"Got to get everyone home in time for dinner, and a drink of water," he added looking at the sweat on the flanks of his horse and the mules.

"Why don't you stop at the stream?"

"I may do that—trouble is, I don't want them to drink too much and they're not going to want to stop once they get in that cold water."

"Yeah, that's what Samantha thought too," Kim laughed. "Well good-bye then. I'll be looking forward to your next visit."

She walked to the edge of the clearing and watched them until they disappeared from sight.

"Darn," she said, putting her hand in her pocket and pulling out a piece of thin plastic tubing. She had found it the night before on her evening walk, and she had meant to ask Jack what it was. Oh well, probably just trash from some litterbug hiker. She stuck it back in her pocket and grabbed the binoculars. There was smoke off to the south.

* * * * * * * *

Saturday, 6 p.m.

"If you're gonna turn that dog loose, I'm waiting in the truck until he's tied back up," Lenny said as Jay drove the truck over the narrow, rutted road to the marijuana field.

"We've got too much work to do for you to be a scaredy-cat. I've told you, that dog won't hurt you unless I tell him to."

Lenny looked unconvinced, but when Jay parked the truck, he cautiously got out and began to carry watering cans down to the stream. As he was filling them, Brutus trotted down to the stream beside him. The panting dog waded chest deep in the water and lapped thirstily.

"Bucket was completely empty—he must have been drinking nonstop for the last two days," Jay said.

Lenny eyed the dog warily, but he seemed to be intent on satisfying his thirst rather than attacking anyone.

"Water the plants at the top of the slope," Jay told him. "There's just not enough water pressure to get the water through the tubing that far. If only the stream were on the other side of the hill, we could snake the tubing over it and let gravity do the rest."

Lenny grunted and picked up two of the heavy watering cans. The bright green of the flourishing plants, now heavy with bud, took his mind off the dog. A few leaves looked wilted, but for the most part, the drip was doing its job except for the very top rows. Some of them were goners, and Lenny kicked the dried-up plants in disgust. But others were salvageable, and he watered those generously.

He joined Jay at the bottom of the slope near the stream. Jay was drinking a beer and smoking a cigarette while Brutus devoured a large bucket of dog food.

"Here," Jay said, handing Lenny a beer from the cooler.

Cautiously, Lenny sat down, still eyeing the dog.

"I made a contact last week in Portland," Jay said sociably.

"Yeah?"

"New customer—more contacts than the one we used last year. I told him we might have some stuff ready by the third week in August if this weather holds."

Lenny drained the last of his beer and reached for another. He silently admitted that Jay had definitely been the brains of the operation, but now his own brain was beginning to think that maybe he ought to learn all aspects of it. After all, he had some plans about striking out on his own one of these days.

"Can I go with you on the drop?"

Jay looked at him and then smiled.

"If you shave and bathe and look like a human being instead of a forest rat."

"Hey! I'm a photographer—remember? I'm high class," Lenny said, laughing. "Gonna win a prize for all my pretty pictures of moss and pine cones and slugs and stuff."

Jay laughed too and for a moment they were just two men sharing a joke over beer on a hot day in the woods.

* * * * * * * *

7 p.m.

Kim walked slowly down the dusty trail. It was too hot to move very fast, but she felt the need to get at least some exercise. Plus, she felt lonely. It was funny that she felt just fine until someone came to visit her. Then when the person left, she keenly felt the absence of human companionship. For now, Jack's cheerful voice and Bart's bark and silly antics filled her thoughts as she walked through the woods.

The trail she usually followed led along the stream, through a ravine, and then over another hill. When she reached the crest of that hill, it was usually getting dark and time to head back to the lookout. Tonight, since she was moving slowly anyway, she decided to take a shorter hike. There was that rock-covered crag she'd been meaning to climb, just to see the view.

Making sure her two-meter rig was secure in her pocket where it wouldn't accidentally fall out, she tackled the rocky surface. The footing seemed pretty secure, and in about 20 minutes, she was near the top. A welcome cool breeze fanned her as she stood on the top and surveyed her domain.

The view was fairly similar to the one from the lookout except that this spot yielded a southeast view of a portion of the valley that was cut off by the hill to the east of her. She pulled her small pocket binoculars from her other pocket and scanned the area with interest.

A brown pickup truck was moving slowly along a logging road through the trees.

"Hmmm," Kim wondered aloud. "Kind of hot for a picnic—wonder what they're doing?"

She shrugged. The summer had taught her that there were all kinds of people in the woods. More than once in the early morning hours, she had heard the sound of baying hounds on an illegal bear hunt. And several rather strange people had stopped in at the lookout, saying they were mushroom hunters.

But by and large, most of the people she met were hikers or fishermen—just common everyday folks out to enjoy the woods. She watched as the brown truck rounded a curve and then disappeared from view, leaving a cloud of dust amongst the fir trees.

Time to get back. There was the schedule with Marc at 9 and then perhaps some DX before bed. But with the hot weather, it was hard to sleep. She might very well wind up sleeping on the catwalk again. Yes, time to get going for sure.

Kim climbed down from her perch and hiked back up to the lookout. The air was definitely cooler now as darkness approached. Maybe, she'd be able to sleep inside after all. She opened the door to the lookout and lit her kerosene lantern. She put her faithful two-meter transceiver and the binoculars beside her bed. There was something else in her pocket. Oh, the piece of plastic tubing she had found.

Strange how that little piece of plastic bothered her. It just didn't seem like something you would find in the woods. She sighed and laid it down on the counter by her book collection.

Chapter 13

19 Candles and 3 Fires

Saturday, August 20th, 5 a.m.
Vista Peak Lookout

The summer was two-thirds over. Where had the last month gone? And now it was her birthday. Kim rolled out of bed and stretched. Nineteen years old! The night before she had taken a shower with water warmed all day in the solar bag. It was a humorous family ritual to take a really good bath the night before a birthday—"washing off all the previous year's dirt," her grandmother used to say.

She smiled thinking of her grandmother, now dead for several years. Kim hoped that sparing shower would have met her requirements. She heated some water on the stove to wash her face and for a quick cup of tea. While it was brewing, she walked out on the deck for her first firewatch of the day.

Late last night, she had heard lookouts reporting a small blaze on the road to Mt. Bachelor just south of Bend. According to reports, the fire had been growing steadily all night, fueled by relentless winds. Kim turned her binoculars to the east and sighed at the black-grey pall that hung over the mountains. Mt. Bachelor was a favorite winter ski resort area, and it saddened her to think of its scenic terrain being blackened.

She listened to Dispatch talking to various lookouts while she French-braided her shoulder length light brown hair into a single braid and fastened it at the nape of her neck with a pink bow. She slipped into navy blue shorts and a bright pink t-shirt. Company was coming! Her parents, her brother Brandon, and Marc. They might be here as early as 8. She hadn't seen Marc in over a month.

Kim scurried around her small home, sweeping the spotless floor one more time. Her mom had said they were bringing everything for her birthday dinner—all she had to do was to try and have some free time to visit with them.

Kim scanned the horizon once again and frowned. The Mt. Bachelor fire was definitely increasing in size. Already, she had heard requests for help to units as far away as Klamath Falls.

She had another, more personal reason, for being concerned about the fire. Marc was leaving here tonight to drive to Sunriver south of Bend for the music festival he had been anticipating all summer. She hoped nothing would get in the way of that.

A tanker plane flew along the edge of the smoke clouds— a silver needle stitching the edge between gray and blue sky. Kim watched the plane bank and head into the smoke to drop its load.

Brandon was the first to reach the lookout. Kim saw him sneaking up the trail and hiding behind some trees. She pretended to be busy watching the south side so that her back was to him as he tiptoed up the steps.

"This is a stickup, m'am," he said putting two fingers to her back.

She jumped and he laughed. Then she hugged him, and he said, "Oh, Kim, don't do that."

"And why not?" she laughed. "Since when have you gotten too big for a hug?"

He gave a quick glance back at the trail to make sure the others weren't in view. Then he gave her a tremendous bear hug of his own. She ruffled his hair and handed him the binoculars.

"Here, you watch for fires. I'll go meet the others."

"Wait!" Brandon sputtered. "What do I do if I see one?"

Kim laughed. She had just scanned the area. By the time, she had gotten across the clearing to the trail, Marc and her parents were coming up the last stretch. This time, there were plenty of hugs and no one seemed embarrassed.

"I've got to hand it to Marc, here," her father said. "I know he wanted to race ahead and be the first to see you, but he hung back and kept us old folks company."

"Who's old? Speak for yourself," Mrs. Stafford said, giving her husband a friendly poke.

"I don't think you would have beaten Brandon anyway. He's been here for 10 minutes," Kim said.

"Hey, Kim, come here!" Brandon yelled.

Kim took the stairs two at a time. Brandon was shaking with excitement, pointing at a white plume off to the northwest near Table Rock. Kim ran inside to get a sighting. She called it in and was surprised that she was the first lookout to spot it.

"Thanks, Brandon, I owe you for that one."

He grinned with pleasure and picked up a second pair of binoculars to scan the other directions.

"He'd better send in an application for a job," Kim said.

Brandon looked at her questioningly to see if she was serious.

"In about five years, Brandon. I think you have to be at least 18. But you'd be a good one—that's for sure."

They watched as the smoke plume enlarged into a dense black area with flickers of orange along the side.

"All those beautiful trees," Mrs. Stafford said sadly. "How can you stand watching them burn, dear."

"I think about how many aren't burning because I'm here," Kim said.

Kim need not have worried about taking time away from her lookout duties to visit. For her birthday, Vista Peak was getting five lookouts. Mr. and Mrs. Stafford, Marc, and Brandon all hung over the railing, intently watching the developing fires.

Kim took a few minutes to stow her mother's goodies in the refrigerator. Cold fried chicken, potato salad, fresh tomatoes, chocolate cake. It all looked so good, her mouth watered. The daily diet of beans and rice she had settled into was satisfying but a little monotonous. She had forgotten what celebration food was like.

The morning passed quickly. Kim pointed out landmarks to her family and showed Brandon how to use the fire finder. All of them watched the Table Rock fire and the Mt. Bachelor fire continue to grow. Now the call was out to every available fire-fighting unit in Oregon to come help, and those in Idaho and Washington were put on alert.

At 11:30, Marc turned to Kim.

"Can you arrange your scans so that you have about ten minutes free at noon? I have a surprise for you."

"Sure. Besides, Brandon will watch."

She smiled at her brother who had not lowered the binoculars once in the time he had been there.

Five minutes before noon, she did an extra careful 360 degree scan of the valleys and mountains.

"If you see anything, yell for me," she told Brandon.

He straightened his shoulders with authority and waved his sister aside. She went in to join Marc at "Jessie," her TS-440 ham radio transceiver.

"Who are you calling?" she asked curiously.

"Just listen," he said, putting his finger to his lips.

"KA7SJP from KH6XM—Happy Birthday Kim!"

Kim gasped and felt a rush of emotion. It was Pete in Maui, the same Pete who had helped in her rescue from bank robbers last winter. With a shaking voice, she replied.

"KH6XM from KA7SJP. Pete! How are you? Oh, it's so good to hear you."

For several minutes, they chatted, reliving past events and sharing new ones. Then Kim saw Brandon waving frantically to her.

"Gotta go, Pete. Thanks so much for calling. KA7SJP clear."

Kim gave the mike to Marc and ran outside to Brandon's side.

"Look," he said.

A new smoke was pluming skyward directly east of them in the direction of Sisters. She ran to get a sighting but Coffin Mountain was already calling it in. Kim backed Coffin Mountain up with a cross shot.

"Oh no," Marc groaned after he signed with Pete and realized what Brandon and Kim were pointing at. "That's exactly the direction I have to go. 'While Nero fiddled, Rome burned.' It looks like while Oregon burned, maybe no one's going to get to fiddle."

"We'll make some phone patches later and find out exactly what's happening," Kim reassured him.

The worry about the fires dampened everyone's enthusiasm for a birthday party. The faint sound of heavy fire trucks moving along Highway 22 was an unhappy accompaniment to their efforts at having a party.

Kim's mother served the food on paper plates.

"We'll pack these down the hill with us, Kim. We didn't want to use any of your precious water doing dishes."

Kim nodded at her thoughtfulness. The chicken dinner tasted delicious. And she couldn't have asked to be surrounded by people she loved more than her family and Marc.

If only there weren't any fires! She chewed thoughtfully on a drumstick as she focused her binoculars on the Table Rock blaze which seemed to be growing by the minute.

"Happy Birthday to you, Happy Birthday to you," Brandon led the singing, carrying the double-layer chocolate cake topped with nineteen flickering candles. He paused in the doorway as a gust of wind put some of them out.

"Here," Kim offered. "I'll come inside to blow them out."

Her mother quickly relighted the pink candles. Kim closed her eyes and made a silent wish. *I wish for all the fires to go out and for everyone fighting them to be safe. And for Marc to get to go to his music festival*, she added. Then she blew out the candles and everyone cheered.

In between bites of cake, she opened the presents they had brought her: some clothing and a beautiful pair of sapphire earrings from her parents; a music tape from Brandon; and a sleek leather-bound diary from Marc with a personal inscription to her on the first page.

"Hey Kim, what's this?" Brandon asked, holding up the thin piece of plastic tubing she had found on the trail.

"I don't know," Kim said. "I found it on one of my walks one night. I meant to ask Jack about it, but I forgot."

Marc held out his hand.

"Let me see that, Brandon."

He took the thin piece of black plastic and examined it closely.

"It's a piece of drip irrigation tubing. My uncle uses this on his Christmas tree farm to water the trees in the summer. Wonder what it's doing up here?"

"Who knows," Kim said. "I see all sorts of strange people up here."

Kim's mother looked worried at that comment, so Kim hastened to reassure her.

"I mean, Mom, someone could be using it as a straw for lemonade, or a lunchbox handle or..."

"Shoe strings or a bean shooter or..." Brandon added laughing.

Marc had moved outside to the railing and was calling a ham in Bend with his two-meter hand-held trying to find out the road conditions.

"It looks like they're going to close Highway 97 at least the rest of the day while they make retardant drops," Marc said unhappily.

"What about the Sunriver Festival?" Kim asked.

"That's what I'm trying to find out now. The guy I just talked to is going to phone and find out for me."

Kim continued watching the fires and monitoring for new smokes. With fires in progress, it was extremely important to watch for any new smokes. The sky in the east continued to blacken, but by three in the afternoon, crews were able to partially contain the Table Rock fire.

Marc finally got the call back he had been waiting for.

"The festival is on," he said. "But no one can get there through Bend. I'm going to have to go south through Eugene and Oakridge and come up through LaPine." He looked at his watch sadly. "Kim, that's about a four hour drive—I guess I need to leave."

Marc had driven his truck separately from the Staffords, so that he could continue on to Sunriver. Kim walked with him across the clearing to the top of the trail.

"Seems like we're always leaving each other," Marc said, taking Kim's face in his hands.

"I know," she said. "But school starts in a little over a month. I hope we can see each other every day then."

"I hope so," Marc laughed, "but I won't plan on it. If this year is anything like last..."

He paused and looked at her and then folded her in his arms.

"You take care, Kim. And remember our sked every day."

Kim blinked back tears.

"I will," she said. "You have fun at the music festival. Make that bass of yours sing."

He kissed her and then turned to go down the trail.

"Happy Birthday!" he shouted as he left her view.

Kim ran back up to the lookout. Her parents were sitting comfortably in deck chairs under the awning while Brandon perched on the railing doing his assumed lookout duties. Kim picked up an extra pair of binoculars and scanned the area. The Table Rock fire was definitely diminishing. Now if only the fire fighters could control the two to the east.

"He's such a nice young man, Kim," her mother said.

"I know," Kim smiled. "I sure hope he gets to Sunriver okay."

"Kim, from what I've seen of Marc, he can get anywhere he sets his mind to. I wouldn't worry about him at all."

Her family stayed until nearly dusk. They snacked on leftovers and then packed up to leave. Kim watched them round the bend, answering their good-byes with shouts of her own.

She thought about going for a quick hike but decided against it. She was tired. It had been quite a birthday. Moving the forestry radio near her bed, she climbed in the bunk and opened the diary from Marc.

"Dear Diary..." she wrote. "Today is my 19th birthday. I had nineteen candles and three fires..."

Chapter 14

Fire Music

Saturday, August 20th 10 p.m.
Sunriver, Oregon

M arc switched on his turn indicator and exited the highway at the Sunriver sign. Even with the windows open, it was still hot in the cab of his truck. He worried about his big bass violin in its leather case and the smaller electric fretless, both lying in the back of the truck. The camper shell had protected them from direct sun, but the extremes of temperature certainly weren't good for these delicate instruments.

He squirted some more windshield cleaner onto the front window. The heavy smoke in the air had made for very poor visibility. He was grateful the long, hot drive was over. There had been many delays due to fire equipment traffic, and Marc had heard some hams on two meters talking about the possibility of Highway 97 being closed to the south as well. He breathed a sigh of relief as he drove by the familiar landmarks of Sunriver and proceeded toward the conservatory area.

Slowly, Marc wound his way along the tree-lined streets. All was dark except for street lights and the fire's eerie red glow off to the north. Marc turned east down a small lane that led to the condominium where the men students would be staying. Right next door to the women's housing.

He knew almost everyone at the festival from various concerts around the state—it would be a fun week. Several cars were parked in front, and Marc nosed his truck into a vacant spot under a tall pine. Lights in the upstairs told him that the other festival participants were still very much awake. Suddenly, he didn't feel tired at all anymore. He grabbed his instruments and hurried inside to greet everyone.

Just as he'd expected, the group was not only up; they were having an impromptu practice session. His longtime friend, Roger, an accomplished cellist from Portland, held his hand up when he saw Marc.

"Hey Buddy—where have you been? We were wondering if you were going to make it."

Marc summarized his eventful day briefly but then started asking questions himself. What about the fire? Was the festival going to continue? Did the conductor from Boston arrive? When were auditions scheduled?

The group laughed at his rapid-fire interrogation, but reassured him. All predictions were that if the winds continued in their present direction, Sunriver was not in any immediate danger. So everything was going to continue as planned. Yes, the conductor was here. All auditions were slated for tomorrow afternoon. Marc smiled, and for the first time that day, felt relaxed. He had been practicing all summer. He could hardly wait for the auditions to determine his placement in the group.

* * * * * * * *

Sunday, August 21st 4 a.m.
Vista Peak Lookout

Kim couldn't imagine why she was awake. It was pitch dark outside. She lay back in her bed and relived the events of her birthday. Really, it had been a pretty great day. How many people got to spend a birthday with loved ones on top of a mountain? A two-meter transmission from Marc later in the evening had reassured her that he had reached his destination safely. She smiled as she thought of him tuning up his instruments and his absolute joy in playing them.

"But why am I awake?" she grumbled to herself.

She turned over and closed her eyes. It was no use. She had never been one to go back to sleep once she woke up.

She flicked on her flashlight and aimed its beam around the room. "Jessie" sat on the counter, beckoning her. Because she had been so tired last night, she had gone to bed without her usual hour of "DXing."

That ought to give me an extra hour of time today, she thought contentedly. She tried closing her eyes again. This time, her enforced rest lasted less than a minute. Shivering in the pre-dawn cool, she got up and slipped into warm sweat-pants and sweatshirt. Without even lighting a lantern, she turned on the transceiver and sat down in front of its friendly lighted dials.

"How about a little CW?" she murmured aloud. "I haven't practiced my code all summer. I'll forget it if I'm not careful."

Carefully, she scanned the CW bands on 20 meters, listening for that odd quality signal that might indicate a faraway station. There was one—very faint.

"••• ——— •••   ••• ——— •••"

S.O.S. S.O.S.! Instantly, Kim was alert. She placed her ear up next to the transceiver, hoping to hear the faint signal more clearly. The signal was starting again. W 6—she couldn't catch the rest of it.

A six signal meant it was probably someone from California, but this sounded so far away. She reached for her key and sent code rapidly to the station asking for a repeat of the information.

Faintly, the signal came back.

"KA7SJP—copy you solid. Am on yacht that has blown off course on trip to Hawaii. Wife very ill. Please notify Coast Guard."

Then the station sent exact latitude and longitude coordinates. Kim copied them down and opened her book of world maps she kept beside the rig. She aimed her flashlight at the page and could just barely make out the location—about 100 miles SW of Kauai.

"Stand by," she sent to the maritime station.

Not much chance of reaching anyone locally on two meters to make a phone call for her at this hour. If she had to, she might find another station on 20 meters to relay for her, but she didn't want to tune the dial away from the distress call. But the Forest Service Dispatch Center could help her.

Kim asked the boat to stand by while she reached for the Forest Service microphone.

"Willamette Dispatch, this is Vista Peak."

"Go ahead, Kim. What's up at this hour?"

"Can you call the Coast Guard for me? There's a boat in trouble 100 miles SW of Kauai."

There was a pause as the dispatcher digested this peculiar information. He was a fairly new dispatcher and didn't know that Kim was an Amateur Radio operator.

"Say what? Do you want to repeat that?"

Quickly, Kim told him how she had come to know this information and emphasized the urgency of the call. As soon as the dispatcher understood the details, he told her to stand by while he placed a phone call to the Coast Guard in Astoria on the north Oregon Coast. Kim paced anxiously around the room, scanning the early dawn horizon with binoculars.

"Vista Peak from Willamette Dispatch."

"This is Vista Peak."

"Your information has been given to the Coast Guard and has been relayed to Pearl Harbor. Rescue vessels will be dispatched immediately. They said to thank you very much."

Kim breathed a sigh of relief but knew she wouldn't really feel easy unless she knew if the yacht was found. And she might never know. She tried calling them again but their signal had faded out completely. She wondered how come she had been the only one to hear the distress call—but stranger things had happened in Amateur Radio. There were always stories of someone's call for help being heard thousands of miles away but not locally. Just one of the many mysteries of bouncing radio waves.

It seemed like she had been on duty for hours already, and yet it was only 6 a.m. Kim ate breakfast and settled into her routine of watching the woods. At 11:30 a.m., her Forest Service radio paged her once again. This time it was Julie, a Dispatcher Kim had gotten to know over the months by their daily brief conversations.

"Vista Peak from Willamette Dispatch."

"This is Vista Peak."

"Kim, I only heard a sketchy outline of what happened this morning with the distress call we relayed. But you'll be happy to know that the Coast Guard in Pearl Harbor just relayed a message through the Astoria Coast Guard to us. Your ailing ship has been rescued. The woman has been taken to the hospital and is doing okay. Both she and her husband, and the Coast Guard send you heartfelt thanks."

"Thank you," Kim said quietly into the microphone, but when she put it down, she stepped outside and let out a whoop of joy.

* * * * * * * *

Sunday, 4 p.m.
The growing field

"What do you think?" Lenny said, holding up one of the marijuana plants which was sagging under the weight of its flowers.

"Just about," Jay said. "Another week for most of the stuff, but I think we can take some now. It's really looking good. Let's get it home and dried, and then we can show our buyer in Portland that we have quality stuff."

Lenny glanced over at Brutus who was watching them hungrily from the end of his chain.

"Feed him, boss. I don't like the way he's looking at me," Lenny said.

"I think I forgot to put his food in," Jay said. "Oh well, I'll bring it tomorrow. Being hungry just makes him a better guard dog."

As Lenny gave the dog a wide berth on the way back to the truck, he noticed that his water bucket was almost empty too. He looked over to Jay to see if he was going to fill it, but Jay was already back to the truck. Lenny ran to join him.

* * * * * * * *

Sunday 5 p.m.
Sunriver

Marc put down his bow and looked at Benjamin Feldstein, the guest conductor for the youth symphony. He had been the last of the five bass players to audition the difficult Haydn piece. Marc felt encouraged that his trained ear told him that he was more skilled than three of the participants. The fourth, a young woman with flaming red hair from Lewis and Clark University in Portland, was probably his equal, if not better. With a slight nod, the conductor motioned her to the first chair and Marc to the second. But then the conductor surprised them both with his words.

"I can't decide between you. So let's have you trade-off. We're performing four pieces. You two can decide which ones you want to sit first chair on."

With a gracious smile, the pretty young bassist turned to Marc and put out her hand.

"Hi, I'm Janet Brinkman. You sounded perfect to me," she said.

"Marc Lawrence. Thank you," he said, shaking her hand and noticing her beautiful green eyes. "So did you. It will be a pleasure performing with you."

After all the positions had been announced, the group broke for dinner. A barbecue had been planned in the large patio area behind the performance hall. The sky was even darker with smoke than it had been the day before.

Marc pulled his two-meter rig from his belt. He had a schedule with Kim at 6 p.m., and he was anxious to hear the official word on the spread of the fires. Several of the other students gathered around him.

"KA7SJP from KA7ITR."

"KA7ITR from KA7SJP. Go ahead Marc."

He said his hellos and let several of his friends visit with Kim while he held the microphone for them.

"What about the fires, Kim? It looks worse down here tonight," Marc asked.

"The skies do look blacker in your direction, Marc, but the official reports are that the fire hasn't moved any closer to your location. The winds are blowing from the east—we're not sure if they're going to be able to save the Mt. Bachelor area or not. And the fire near Sisters is spreading both east and northward. You see, it jumped Highway 20—that road has been closed all day."

The students listened to this news somberly. This week-long music festival was supposed to be a happy time. It was something all of them had looked forward to and practiced for all summer. Official rehearsals wouldn't begin until tomorrow with a final performance the following Saturday.

"I bet they get it out by tomorrow," Roger said.

Janet looked at the ashen sky.

"I sure hope so," she said doubtfully.

* * * * * * * *

The next two days were a push and pull battle between the fiery forces of nature and the determined ones of man. The fires grew slowly, eating the dry tinder and exploding with insatiable hunger toward each new patch of fuel. The weary men and women, on the ground and in the sky, fought the fire beast with shovels, water, chemicals, and sheer human will.

In some places, the fire backed off, flickering with resentment toward those who would contain it. At other locations, it forged rapidly ahead of its human hunters, leaving them behind.

The many homes and ranches in the areas near Mt. Bachelor and the town of Sisters were evacuated. Residents, carrying hurriedly gathered belongings, flocked to temporary emergency shelters in Bend. Anxiously, they listened to TV and radio reports—waiting to see who would win the battle.

* * * * * * * *

Wednesday, August 24th 4 p.m.
Sunriver

"B flat," Conductor Feldstein shouted at a second violinist. "I don't know what's wrong with this group. We only have two days until the performance, and it sounds like you're all still going through it for the first time."

He put down his baton and walked to the doorway angrily. The scream of fire engines in the distance echoed into the room. Ash was fluttering down from the sky, littering the walkways. He shut the door and walked back to the group.

"Okay," he said a little more patiently, tapping the music stand with a pencil. "Once more from the beginning of the second movement."

The young musicians leaned into their tasks with renewed energy. A long picture window on the side of the building framed the angry skies. Unconsciously, they began to quicken the tempo, and the conductor joined them, his baton marking the accelerated rhythm. "Hurry, hurry, hurry," the music seemed to say.

Chapter 15

To Market, to Market...

Thursday, August 25th, 8 a.m.
Silverton

J ay eased the rickety barn door open and slipped inside. This barn had definitely seen better days, but it was perfect for their use. Roomy, well ventilated, wired for electricity, and best of all: hidden from the road. The sweet, pungent smell of drying marijuana wafted through the warm air, and Jay inhaled deeply. That was the smell of money.

The large leaves had been hanging from the rafters for three days now. By opening the windows in the hayloft and setting up a couple of fans, Jay had accelerated the drying process. Lenny sure hadn't been much help. The lady redhead at the tavern never came back, but apparently Lenny had managed to strike up a friendship with an alcoholic blonde. Out until three last night, he was still snoring away in the house. Well, he'd better get himself up. They had work to do!

Jay stepped over the power cords of the fans and left the barn. He banged the screen door behind him as he went into the kitchen. Lenny's cavernous snores filled the whole house. With a grin, Jay picked up a mildewed wet rag lying on the kitchen floor where someone had dropped it several days ago. He ran it under the icy-cold well water from the kitchen tap.

"Time to rise and shine, Romeo," Jay said, hurling the drippy, smelly towel across the room into Lenny's sleeping face.

"What the!" Lenny yelled, jumping from the bed. He pivoted right and left, looking for the enemy, but his eyes were still shut. Then he opened them slowly and saw Jay standing in the doorway grinning at him. Lenny grabbed his head, moaned, and fell back on the bed.

"Had a good time last night, I can see," Jay said. "Well, we've got a very important date tonight in Portland—a lot more important than you'll ever find in that tavern, so get your louse-ridden self up and come out to help me."

* * * * * * * *

Thursday, August 25th 9 a.m.
Vista Peak

Kim stood on the east side of the lookout platform, squinting through the binoculars, trying to see through the heavy smoke hanging over the Bend/Sunriver area to the east. A change in the winds had turned the front of the fire during the night. Now it was sweeping fiercely toward the south. Sunriver was directly in its path.

Ironically, all was quiet on the western front. The valley floors and mountain peaks near Vista Peak hadn't produced even one "smoke" during the last two days. Kim hoped people reading about the inferno raging along the eastern slope of the Cascades, were being careful in the woods.

All of the lookouts were extra attentive. With the state's fire-fighting resources badly strained by the two fires near Bend, it was vital that no new fire get a foothold anywhere.

At noon came the dreaded news that the "Sisters Fire" and the "Mt. Bachelor Fire" had merged into one. Instead of two fire-breathing dragons, the crews were now fighting one. Generating its own winds, the one quickly became much bigger than the sum of the two. Newscasters dubbed it the "Cascade Inferno," and the title was appropriate. Thirty-nine more homes fell victim to its appetite and 11 firefighters were hospitalized with burns and smoke inhalation.

"KA7SJP from KA7ITR"

One o'clock—schedule with Marc.

"KA7ITR from KA7SJP. Go ahead Marc," Kim said anxiously.

Marc's voice sounded strained.

"It doesn't look good, Kim. The directors of the festival said they'll wait one more hour, but we're all making plans to leave. Can I check back with you in thirty minutes? Things are pretty crazy around here."

"Sure, Marc. I'm so sorry. Just make sure you all get moving in time. This one's a real beast."

"Roger, Kim. Got to go. KA7ITR clear."

"KA7SJP clear."

Kim shook her fist at the black sky.

"You kill animals, you consume homes, you incinerate forests, and now you're destroying beautiful music...but don't you dare hurt the people, you hear!"

Kim wiped her eyes and walked over to the west side to watch her valley.

* * * * * * * *

Thursday 9:20 a.m.
Sunriver

"I'm sorry," Conductor Feldstein said to the impromptu gathering of students in the dining hall. "We've all got to be out of here in the next half hour. We considered the possibility of waiting this out somewhere, but the fire chief I talked to said it would probably be days before any of us would be allowed back in the area."

There was a large moan from the musicians.

"Look, all I can say is that we're going to perform these pieces. I'm not sure when, but I have all of your phone numbers and we'll arrange a time when everyone can meet during the year. Now, let's get moving. Each of you must check in with me before leaving," the conductor said, holding up a list of their names. "We have several carpools going south. That's the safest way, but Highway 97 north is open at the moment. There's a forest ranger here who has offered to lead a caravan of anyone wanting to go to Bend. From there, he'll give you directions on the best routes to get home."

Marc looked over at Forest Ranger Kyle Thomas who happened to be N7IBV. He had met him the night before when several fire and forest service officials had come to the resort to discuss evacuation plans.

"How many do you think want to go north?" Kyle asked Marc.

"Just four of us, I think."

"Okay, there's one small section of the main highway that has been closed off and on due to air tanker runs, but we can take an alternate road. Right now, the fire is west of the highway, but that could change quickly. So anyone who wants to go north had better do so now."

Marc loaded his things hastily. There wasn't time for real good-byes, but students yelled to each other and reached out for quick hand clasps as they ran to pack. Marc closed the back of his truck, then drove over to Cottonwood Street where he was to meet Kyle Thomas and three other students who had brought their cars. One of those was Janet Brinkman who was trying to get back to Portland. Riding with her was her younger sister, Cecily, a violinist. Kyle was going to lead the procession and Marc would follow. Kyle would be in touch with the Forest Service Dispatch on his radio. If there were any abrupt changes in the fire, he could relay to Marc on two meters.

The hot smoky air stung Marc's eyes as he swung into line at the end of the procession.

"KA7SJP from KA7ITR"

"Go ahead, Marc. This is KA7SJP."

"Bad news is we're leaving," Marc said, taking a deep breath. "Good news is that if I can get through on Highway 20, I was thinking about coming up to spend the day with you."

"Last I heard that road was open," Kim said. "And it will be great to see you. Just be careful, okay?"

Marc signed clear and squinted his eyes against the soot-laden air assaulting him. They traveled through an area that had already been burned. What once had been a scenic roadside dotted with fragrant sagebrush, juniper and green Jack pine was now a desolate, charred landscape, evidence of a battle lost against one of man's worst enemies. Marc gripped the steering wheel tighter and concentrated on the difficult drive ahead, trying not to look at the black skeletons of trees that bordered the highway.

* * * * * * * *

Thursday 4 p.m.
Silverton

"You call that shaving?" Jay snarled at Lenny.

Lenny rubbed his hand across the blond stubble on his face.

"Razor's dull," he muttered.

"Well, take one of mine or else I'll shave you myself with a chainsaw. Remember, we're going to Portland to meet the buyer, or hasn't that fact sunk into your thick brain? We have to look like executives, not bums."

Lenny grumbled and moved toward the bathroom. Twenty minutes later, he reappeared. His blue slacks were slightly rumpled and a grease stain was obvious on one leg. But the white shirt and black tie he wore appeared fairly clean. Jay looked at him appraisingly, then grunted approval.

"Okay, let's get loaded," he said.

The two of them had spent the midday carefully wrapping and double wrapping the compressed marijuana leaves into four- by eight- by twelve-inch brown-plastic kilo bags. They'd concealed these neatly in two store shopping bags inside one of the bench compartments of their truck pickup bed. Loose work clothes were strewn over the bags.

Jay put his chainsaw and a can of gasoline in the back. At first glance, they simply were two men who had their wood-cutting supplies along with them for a proposed firewood expedition the next day.

"Okay, let's go," Jay said to Lenny.

At five p.m. it was 100 degrees in the hillside town of Silverton. Both men were sweating by the time they got everything ready to go.

"I hope you wore deodorant," Jay said to Lenny, wrinkling his nose in disgust.

"You're no rosebud," Lenny retorted, slamming the truck door shut.

They were silent as they drove along the wheatfield-edged road that connected to Interstate 5. With the windows down and the roar of freeway traffic, there was no need for shouted conversation. Jay swung up the onramp and settled back in his seat.

He had never dealt with these Portland men before. Didn't even know their names. He'd been given the code name "cigar," and told they would meet him in the back parking lot of a well-known shopping center in the city. Jay was supposed to park his truck by a dumpster at the southeast corner and wait. He sweated nervously as he thought about the upcoming meeting.

Lenny's snores interrupted his thoughts. *Incredible*, thought Jay. *The guy can sleep anywhere.*

* * * * * * * *

Thursday, 7 p.m.
Sisters, Oregon

Marc drove wearily into the small mountain town of Sisters, west of Bend. He had just spent the last seven hours waiting in Bend for word that Highway 20 was open to the west. The two other cars of students had been able to head directly north to Portland via Madras, Warm Springs, and the Mt. Hood Loop.

There had only been time for a hasty good-bye to Janet and Cecily. Marc and Janet exchanged phone numbers, promising to call each other on the weekend to assure each other of their safe arrival home.

After their departure, Marc had spent the hot, smoky day walking through shopping malls and talking to Kim briefly every hour. He wished he could have talked to her more, but Kim needed to watch her battery time. Fortunately, Marc was able to run his two-meter rig directly off the car battery. Kim needed to recharge hers with solar power.

Marc bypassed a couple of new movies playing in the mall because he wanted to keep monitoring the highway situation in case there was a chance of getting through earlier. When the word finally came at 6:30, that vehicles were being allowed through, he was first in line.

And now here he was in the small town of Sisters, famous for its antique shops. Longtime family friends lived near the city park. Like many residents, Mr. and Mrs. Peterson owned and operated a small antique business. Dave, their son, who had gone to grade school with Marc, was now in the Navy. Marc had called the Petersons as soon as he drove into Sisters. They promptly invited him to dinner and for the night.

"I want to leave by 8 or 9 tomorrow morning so I can stop and see a friend who's working as a lookout this summer," Marc told them. "I don't know what time you get up, but don't change your schedule for me."

"Nonsense," Mr. Peterson laughed. "I get up with the birds—in fact, earlier than a lot of them. Eight o'clock is the middle of the day to me. You rise and shine whenever you want. I'll have breakfast cooking."

Marc sat back and smiled happily. After the stresses and disappointments of the last few days, it felt good to be taken care of with parently concern.

The Petersons had lots of questions about what he had been doing and how his family was. They sat and talked late into the evening. It was midnight when Marc finally crawled into bed. As he closed his eyes, he wondered sleepily if he would wake up "with the birds" as Mr. Peterson said.

* * * * * * * *

Midnight
Marijuana Field

Brutus was awake and panting. Once again, the hunger and thirst demons had joined his body. His muscles twitched restlessly. Before when he had been so hungry, it had been because the man hadn't come with food. But now, the man had been there and hadn't brought him food. He hadn't even looked at him. Brutus's dog brain didn't understand. But his instinct told him that he needed food and water to survive. His neck was worn raw from constant pulling on the chain.

There was no escape. With a sigh, he settled back on his haunches and waited.

Chapter 16

Evil in the Night

Thursday, August 25th, 9 p.m.
Parking lot in Portland

"Y ou sure you didn't spill any of that catsup on your front?" Jay questioned Lenny as they drove back to the parking lot they had checked out earlier.

Lenny looked down at his white shirt, now limp with moisture from his perspiring body.

"Nope, clean as a whistle. I feel kind of sick though—three orders of French fries. Why'd we come so early anyway? First you drive over here to find the dumpster—it's there all right just like the guy said. So what do we have to do? Go kill an hour eating burgers and fries. In this heat, I feel like my gut's been attacked by gremlins."

"You get sick and I'll leave you behind in that dumpster," Jay growled.

Lenny looked over at him to see if he was serious. Jay was concentrating on the parking lot, looking nervously right to left to see if anyone would think it strange that two men were driving toward a trash dumpster at 9 p.m. The shopping mall had just closed and the lights of cars leaving the lot formed a red chain which stretched for nearly a city block. Jay parked about 20 feet away from the gray metal trash container.

"Supposin' the cops come," Lenny queried nervously. "I mean everyone else is leaving the place—what's our excuse for parking here? We like to look at trash?"

Jay had barely said "shut up" to Lenny when a newer-model black sedan drove up opposite them. In the dim light, Jay and Lenny could barely see the two men inside. The driver rolled down his window and asked congenially, "How about a cigar?"

"Sure thing," Jay said. "Just a minute. I keep them in the back."

Lenny waited in the front seat anxiously while Jay walked around to the back of the truck, opened the camper shell, and retrieved the two shopping bags from beneath the bench seat. He handed them to the man who rapidly deposited them in the sedan's trunk.

"I'll call you at home in two hours to let you know if we want the order," he said to Jay.

Then the man got back in his car and they drove away quickly. Jay came back to the truck cab.

"Well?" Lenny asked.

"They'll call at 11. They have to go someplace and check the stuff, you know. I'm not worried. That's prime pot. They'll want it, I guarantee."

Jay stepped on the accelerator, and soon they joined the line of exiting cars, filled with tired shoppers and parcels. Lenny leaned his head against the door frame and went to sleep.

* * * * * * * *

Thursday, 10 p.m.
Vista Peak

Kim signed with Marc and climbed into bed. What an adventure he'd had! Thankfully, he was now safe in Sisters, and tomorrow he would be visiting her for part of the day before heading back home to Portland. How sad that the music festival had been cancelled, but that unhappiness was nothing compared to the tragedy of the dozens of people who had lost their homes due to the Cascade Inferno. Kim felt an overwhelming wave of sadness for them as she closed her eyes and tried to sleep.

* * * * * * * *

Friday, August 26th
1 a.m.

Fifteen miles southwest of Kim's lookout, a man named Earl Risto, slumbered under the stars. At age 56, it was his first fishing trip alone. Always before, he'd come with buddies or his wife. This time, his wife was in California visiting relatives, and all of his fishing friends had other plans. But when the fishing bug bit Earl, he went fishing. Sweltering away in Albany in 100 plus temperatures, he'd taken an extra day off from work and proceeded into the mountains.

Sitting on the edge of the cool stream, Earl thought that even though the fishing bug might have bitten him, the fish in the stream definitely weren't biting his line. After five hours of trying, he was just about to give up and eat cold sandwiches when a trout struck his line. Within seconds, Earl had the wriggling fish on shore, off the hook, and in his wicker basket. However, another hour of trying didn't lead to anything more than relaxation, so Earl decided to call it quits. He built himself a small campfire to roast his newly caught dinner. With some French bread, fresh fruit, and cold beer he'd brought from home, he had himself a handsome meal. After carefully putting out his campfire, he unrolled his sleeping bag, slid in, and lay back to watch the stars.

"Now, this is living," Earl said aloud. "Just wish I had someone here to share it with though."

Sleep eluded him, so he reached over to his backpack and grabbed a cigarette. Tobacco had always been a pretty good companion when no one else was around. For years, Earl had been promising his wife he'd quit, and in truth, he rarely did smoke anymore. Tonight, though, seemed to warrant a cigarette. He lit it and settled on his back, watching his smoke drift into the black night. Soon, he was growing sleepy, and with a half-hearted twist of his wrist, he ground out the cigarette in the dirt and fir needles beside him.

At least, he thought it was out. It wasn't. The tiny ember of flame from the cigarette butt grew during the next hour by feeding on dry fir and hemlock needles. Earl snored, lost in a void of sleep. A gust of warm wind caught the small glowing embers and tossed them over into a larger pile of brush a few feet from Earl. Another hour passed, and the fire barely survived. Just an occasional small pop or wisp of smoke told of its existence. But it was laying groundwork. The fire's fuel—piles and piles of dry needles, leaves, and twigs were gradually heating to the ignition flash point. A gust of air, so slight that it barely ruffled Earl's hair, breathed life into the embers, and suddenly, it ignited!

With a start, Earl woke up to the loud crackling noise and stinging smell of smoke. Fire! A whole clump of brush was burning wildly just a few feet from him. He jumped up and began beating frantically at the flames with his shirt. The shirt immediately caught fire, and Earl dropped it.

He grabbed his bait bucket and clambered barefoot down to the stream in his underwear. By the time, the frantic fisherman got back to his campsite, the fire had quadrupled and was racing up some of the bone dry trees, sending showers of sparks into the air.

His shovel! He had to get his shovel from the truck, but the truck was parked some 30 yards above him on the edge of the embankment. Even as he raced up the rocky slope, Earl knew he was fighting a losing battle. The fire had become a beast, expanding faster than he could ever have imagined. Its growing roar was in his ears as he reached the truck and pulled open the canopy door. Just then one of the trees "candled," exploding skyward into a huge fiery ball. Shaking, Earl ran back to the truck cab and climbed in. Realizing that he'd left his pants and shoes back at the campsite, he fumbled under the seat for the extra set of keys.

With trembling fingers, he started the truck and raced down the road. It was twenty miles to the first pay phone. Earl stopped and called 911, but news of the fire had already been received. A private pilot flying from Klamath Falls to Portland had been the first to spot it and radio the information to the control tower in Portland. Minutes later, calls started coming in from all over.

* * * * * * * *

If anyone had asked Earl Risto how he felt about the Spotted Owl controversy that embroiled the Northwest and other parts of the nation in the late eighties and early nineties, he would have shrugged his shoulders and said, "Oh, I dunno, there's two sides to it, I guess." Environmentalists, trying to save the habitat of this endangered species called the Spotted Owl, pitted themselves against the logging industry of the Northwest. At stake was old growth timber, an economic base and livelihood for many towns and people, but also habitat for the Spotted Owl.

Environmentalists staged protests where they chained themselves to trees. Unemployed loggers drove their empty log trucks through major cities in parades of unrest. Jobs versus birds. The debate grew as heated as a forest fire.

Earl Risto, in one moment of carelessness, settled the argument for one area of the Cascade wilderness. As the fire he had caused grew and grew, it swept into Spotted Owl territory and rapidly consumed the trees that had been the subject of controversy. Now, no one would have them—neither winged fowl nor human beast.

* * * * * * * *

Friday, 4 a.m.
Detroit Ranger Station

"We've got another big one on our hands," U.S. Forest Incident Commander Leo Bernaldi told his subordinates in the middle of the night. Distant fire-fighting crews were on their way, but the manpower of the Northwest was already overtaxed with the raging Cascade Inferno. Calls went out to Idaho, Colorado, Utah, Wyoming, California, and Nevada. In the pre-dawn, fire fighters from many areas of the west hurried to airports to catch flights for Portland, Oregon where they would be transported to the fire zones.

Not since the devastating Yellowstone fire of '88, had the potential for disaster been so great. It wasn't so much the size of this new "Santiam Fire" that worried officials. Many bigger blazes had been successfully contained in a day or two. It was the speed with which this one was growing that scared everyone. And the weather reports were dismal. Strong winds from the northeast were expected to increase as temperatures soared over the next few days.

Bernaldi alerted the Air Tanker Center in Redmond to be ready to fly at first light. Already, he was scanning his list of backup tanker centers in nearby states. They were going to need everything they could get!

The Santiam Highway, called Highway 22 on the Salem side of the mountains, and Highway 20 after it intersects with Highway 20 six miles west of the Santiam Junction, became a busy corridor before daybreak. For the moment, regular traffic was still being allowed through since the fire was far from the road. But, it was slow going for anyone traveling through. Fire vehicles passed cars, and the highway was clogged with many support vehicles—many of them carrying supplies for the weary fire fighters.

When the first relief crew arrived at the northern tip of the fire, they found exhausted men and women, some of whom had already been battling the "Cascade Inferno" for days. Gratefully, the tired fighters got into vehicles that transported them to nearby camps where they could sleep and eat. Most fell asleep seconds after they sat down in the transport vehicles.

* * * * * * * *

Earl Risto continued on home. The Dispatch Operator who had taken the fire information from him had asked his name, address, and phone number. Earl tried to remember what he had said. Had he told her that the fire started at his campsite? That it must have been from his campfire or cigarette? Well, maybe he hadn't started it. Earl tried very hard to rationalize as he drove toward home. Perhaps there had been a lightning strike. But Earl had heard no thunder, and the skies were clear. He ran other possibilities through his mind, but none seemed plausible.

Several fire trucks passed him on the road to Albany, and he pulled over each time. In his rearview mirror, the dawning sky was a brilliant orange red as the sunlight tried to break through the increasing clouds of smoke. As the enormity of what he had caused began to sink in, Earl started to shake. Pretty soon, tears came to his eyes and he pulled over to the side of the road and sobbed.

* * * * * * * *

Friday 5 a.m.
Vista Peak

All of the lookouts were alerted as soon as the growing fire was reported and asked to verify its location. For some reason, Kim suddenly woke up moments before she was called. During the summer months, the glass windows had made her very light sensitive. She woke precisely at the first ray of light. This morning, she sat up and inhaled deeply. Smoke! Immediately, she was out on the catwalk. A bright-orange glow southwest of her shimmered in the distance. She guessed it was at least 10 to 15 miles away, but its eerie dancing light looked as though it were reaching out for her.

She dressed quickly and checked in with her superiors at Dispatch. All lookouts in the vicinity were told to closely monitor the progress of the fire and give as much new information as possible to the people directing the fire-fighting units.

As the sky began to lighten, Kim heard the familiar roar of the air tankers. She watched as the C130 followed by the DC7 flew toward the dancing lights and began to drop their loads.

Chapter 17

A Matter of Time

Friday, August 26th, 6 a.m.
In the skies above the Santiam Fire

For two years, a giant C130A, better known to fire crews as Tanker 67, had been part of the arsenal that the Redmond Air Center used to combat fire. The huge 120,000-lb cargo plane had been traded from the military which was no longer using the C130A.

A C123 and some helicopters went to an aeronautical museum, and the C130—soon labeled Tanker 67—came home to roost in Redmond. Some special modifications in the belly of the aircraft had turned it into a valuable weapon against the forces of fire.

Now at 6 a.m., copilot Lance Rettig, KB7NLD, looked through the window by his right knee down at the "slurry" drop they had just completed from Tanker 67. It had been a full drop or "salvo" of 3000 gallons of the ammonium phosphate mixture in 66 seconds. As the 27,000 pounds of fire retardant left the aircraft, the sudden change in weight caused its nose to pitch up slightly. Pilot Sil Myers corrected immediately.

"What do you think?" he asked Lance.

"Looks like we cooled the edge some," Lance replied. "Mike's right behind us dropping his."

Mike Lewis was the pilot of Tanker 66, a DC7, well known in Oregon for its fire service record. Tanker 66 and 67 had been able to handle all fires in past seasons, but the pilots had already heard that reinforcements had been called to battle the dual threat of the Santiam Fire and the Cascade Inferno. Even with their impressive reloading time, two tankers were literally going to be a drop in the bucket against these blazes.

"Doesn't look like you're going to have any time for that ham radio of yours, today," Sil half chuckled as they headed back to the Redmond Air Base.

Lance's love of Amateur Radio was well-known on the base. He never went anywhere without at least one radio. On board the C130, he kept a two-meter rig tucked under his seat. He had attached an antenna to the window of the plane and linked the small transceiver to his headset so he could hear transmissions above the aircraft noise.

On rare occasions, he had time to contact another station while in the air. It was precisely for those occasions that he always kept the rig ready with its battery pack charged. What a kick he got out of an Amateur Radio operator's surprise when hearing him come back with his airborne location.

Today, there would be no time for "hamming." Lance concentrated on the controls that closed the airplane's belly after the fire retardant had exited. Cruising at 250 knots (287 mph), it took them only minutes to return to the base. The loading crew was waiting, ready to replenish the precious fire-stopping liquid retardants. Soon, they were airborne and returning once again to the Santiam Fire.

* * * * * * * *

Friday, 7 a.m.
Silverton

"Hurry!" Jay yelled at Lenny who was sitting dazed-looking on the edge of his bed.

"Hurry? What for?" Lenny said in a sleepy voice.

"Look—that's what," Jay said, pointing out the kitchen window on the east side of the room.

Lenny ambled slowly over to the window and squinted in the bright morning light. The entire horizon was black with huge black and gray clouds plummeting skyward.

"Where is it?" he asked Jay solemnly.

"I'm not sure, exactly. Somewhere in the Santiam Canyon, but the radio said the fire is moving rapidly North-east. Come on, we've got to get the plants."

Lenny didn't protest. Just as Jay had predicted, the call had come in last night from "Cigar," saying they would pay cash on delivery for the harvest. Jay and Lenny had planned to take several days to clear the area. Even with drying time, they had calculated that by this time next week, they would be rich. Last night, they had sat up late, sharing a case of beer, talking about how each of them would spend his new wealth.

Now, it looked like Mother Nature could turn their cash crop to ashes. Silently, Lenny threw on some clothes and ran to join Jay who was standing out by the truck rubbing his chin thoughtfully.

"We can't take a chainsaw in there. If they let us through, and that's a big if, I'm sure there's no woodcutting being allowed anywhere. So that excuse won't work."

"What about the photography bit?" Lenny asked.

"No, I think we need something more urgent than that—if they're just letting some traffic through, we need a reason to be in that traffic."

"How are we going to conceal the stuff even if they do let us in?" Lenny asked.

"Cover it with hay, I guess," Jay answered. "Here grab some of those bales."

Lenny looked doubtful.

"You know, going to jail isn't what I've been looking forward to all summer," he muttered.

"Look, it'll work," Jay said, kicking a clod of loose dirt. "We tell them we're taking the hay to a brother who lives near Sisters. We'll say his truck has broken down, and he needs the hay real bad. Then we can use the hay to cover the plants on the way out. We won't risk coming back home the same way—if 20's open to Albany, we'll go that way—otherwise, we'll have to travel on to Bend and circle up through Portland."

"I don't like it, I don't like it all," Lenny complained. "That's a lot of miles on the road—a lot of miles where someone can stop us and see what's in the back."

"You got any better ideas?"

Lenny was quiet. The two of them loaded the hay and then jumped in the truck to head toward the smoke-shrouded Cascades. As the miles zipped by, they both riveted their attention on the building wall of smoke ahead. Fire truck after fire truck passed. Each time, Jay drew over to the right side of the road and waited patiently for the vehicle to pass. And each time, Lenny shook his head, whistled through his teeth, and said, "I dunno, Boss. I dunno."

They reached Mill City. The skies got blacker but there were no roadblocks. They reached Detroit Dam with its banks much lower this summer due to the drought. The little town of Detroit was buzzing with activity—emergency vehicles of every sort were parked along the roadside as worried officials from every agency conferred. Two miles beyond Detroit was the roadblock that Lenny was so afraid of. A State Highway Department employee had his truck parked sideways, partially blocking the northbound traffic. A sheriff's deputy stood nearby as backup. The southbound lane was open with a trickle of cars going through.

"Let me handle this," Jay warned Lenny as he came to a stop.

"Good morning," the uniformed highway worker said pleasantly. "What's your destination?"

"Sisters," Jay said calmly. "My brother needs some hay pretty bad, and his truck's broken down."

The deputy looked at him evenly.

"We can let you through now, but there's no guarantee you can get back. If the wind keeps going the same direction on this fire, we anticipate the flames might reach the road this afternoon."

"Oh, sorry to hear that," Jay said, "but it's no big deal if we can't get back today. We wanted to spend the night with my brother anyway. How's that fire doing over near Bend?"

"No problem in Sisters now," the deputy said. "The main blaze is way south of there. The road's open all the way to Bend. You could get back by going up through Portland if you had to, but it'd be a long trip."

"My cousin and I were just talking about maybe doing that anyway," Jay said, half gesturing at Lenny. "Been a long time since we been to Portland."

"Okay," the deputy said, waving them through. "Just don't stop for anything and be careful."

He stood in the road watching their truck disappear. Some instinct made him write their license down and then he wondered why he had. There wasn't really anything suspicious about the guys other than they obviously needed a bath. He felt sorry for the brother they were going to visit.

* * * * * * * *

"We're safe," Jay whooped as they drove out of view of the roadblock. "And look—the fire's definitely still south of the road. Our plot's safe, but we'd better hurry. No telling how long our luck will last."

He reached the logging road they always used, making sure no other vehicle was in sight before turning in. The orange flag that someone had hung from a lower branch of a fir tree had become a familiar landmark to them both. Jay pushed the gas pedal down, and Lenny grunted and gasped as Jay hit the bumps in the road.

"Hey, watch it!" he complained loudly.

"Like I said, we don't have any time to waste," Jay retorted, accelerating even more.

Lenny clung to the door handle. Finally, the going got so rough that Jay was forced to slow down and ease his way through potholes. Both of them wiped their eyes, smarting from the smoke. Jay drove the truck careening into the small clearing and jumped out. Brutus was standing there, panting, watching them expectantly. The men didn't even see him. They grabbed machetes and ran to the plants.

After an hour, they were both sweating heavily, and less than ten percent of the plants had been harvested.

"This is rough with them so spread out," Lenny complained.

"Just keep cutting and keep stuffing them into the truck bed," Jay ordered. "I doubt we're going to get a chance at a second load, so let's cram as much in as we can."

Lenny stopped a minute by the creek to soak his grease-stained handkerchief in the cold water and mop his face. But then Jay yelled at him to get busy, so he ran back up the hill to resume cutting.

"Mexico, Baja—that's where I'm going," Lenny told himself aloud as he labored. "Big sandy beaches, cold beer, lobster."

Suddenly, he didn't feel so hot anymore and he tackled the plants with renewed vigor.

* * * * * * * *

Vista Peak 9 a.m.

It was the first time Kim had really felt afraid. Even in the thunderstorm and the subsequent fire that caused her evacuation, she felt in control of the situation. Now, as she watched the billowing towers of smoke moving toward her and sensed the controlled urgency in the voices of those commanding the fire-fighting forces, she felt very uneasy.

"KA7SJP from KA7ITR."

"KA7ITR from KA7SJP. Good morning, Marc—where are you?"

"I'm still in Sisters. More important, how are you? I just woke up about an hour ago and heard about the fire. How close is it to you?"

"Seven to eight miles, I think, Marc. It's hard to tell. This one's definitely moving fast. I've never seen anything like it."

Marc sounded worried. "Are you safe, Kim?"

"Oh sure, don't worry about me. If it gets really close, they'll evacuate the lookouts. I'm not sure if you're going to want to come up here or not, though. I'll not have any time to visit. In fact, I'm scanning with binoculars as I talk to you now."

"Look, Kim," Marc said after a pause. "I'm going to leave now. Mr. Peterson just called the Ranger Station here in

129

Sisters and found out that the road is still open. Could you have a schedule with me at 9:30 and again at 10? By 10, I should be about to your trail. Let's see how things are going."

"Okay," Kim said, sounding doubtful. "I just really don't know..."

There was a pause.

"Kim?"

"I'm here. The fire just jumped some sort of road down there. Trees are actually exploding—I've never seen anything like it. Oh, I hope the fire crews are okay—someone's giving orders on the radio right now to move an entire line of fighters."

Marc could hear the rapid talk on her Forest Service radio in the background. Coupled with the din of heavy equipment going past the Petersons' house, he felt his own anxiety rise.

"Kim, listen. I know you need to save batteries. But I'll leave my rig on this frequency the whole way. If anything changes, let me know. Hey, I just had a thought. In case you do have to leave later today, would you like me to hike up now and carry some of your equipment out?"

"We'll see," Kim said. "This thing's really getting big. They're estimating over 4000 acres already. I don't want you coming up here unless it's safe. If I have to leave, it's going to be in a big hurry. Oh, Marc, if only those winds would change!"

Chapter 18

Walls of Fire

Highway 20
Friday, August 26th, 9:30 a.m.

Marc sat impatiently, drumming his fingers on the steering wheel. He looked in his rearview mirror at the five cars behind him. There had been ten, but when the sheriff's deputy told the waiting drivers that it could be as much as thirty minutes more before a disabled water tanker truck would be removed from the highway a mile ahead, many of the drivers had opted to turn around and go back toward Sisters.

"KA7SJP from KA7ITR"

No answer.

"KA7SJP from KA7ITR. Kim?"

"KA7ITR from KA7SJP. Sorry, Marc, I was talking to Dispatch. This is getting very bad. I would advise you not to come. I may be leaving here soon."

"I understand, Kim. I'm stuck here right now, but if they open the road, I'm driving your way. Let's just plan it as it happens, okay?"

"Roger, Marc—gotta go—monitor for me. KA7SJP clear."

* * * * * * * *

9:45 a.m.

The more the Santiam Fire consumed, the hungrier it became. Devouring old growth and second-growth timber alike, the fire swept through the canyons and up the hillsides. Deer, coyote, bear, and elk ran panic-stricken ahead of the flames. For those who made a wrong turn, death was instant and horrible. For the many smaller animals and birds caught in their burrows and nests, there was no time to try to flee. The fire swept them into its consuming force and continued on its way relentlessly.

Fire lines were moved back like armies in hasty retreat. No time now to directly assault the flames. Instead, crews shoveled frantically, trying to clear fire breaks ahead of the blaze. If only they could circle it and stop its march. With determination and flying skill, the aerial tankers dropped load after load of slurry on the edge of the inferno, trying to slow its progress. Crews on the ground sprayed white foam retardant on brushy areas not yet burned.

But the fire was not to be denied. When man's efforts squelched its heat in one area, it reached out flaming tentacles to another and burned with increased fury. And to broadcast its power over an even wider range, it sent burning sparks sailing on the wind to new places where they touched down to start new smaller fires. One of them landed directly east of Vista Peak, and a few trees were burnt before a slurry drop snuffed it out.

* * * * * * * *

"It's getting closer to us, boss. I can hear it," Lenny said.

The roar of exploding trees and igniting timber filled the air. Ashes rained down steadily now, and both Jay and Lenny tied their handkerchiefs over their mouths and noses in an attempt to filter the air. Brutus lay on the ground, coughing and whimpering occasionally.

Jay was up in the truck bed, stomping the valuable leaves down into crevices while Lenny handed him even more plants. Jay opened the seat along the side and crammed this latest batch in there.

"Okay, one more layer—let's go get some from the top of the hill."

"No way," Lenny protested. "Look!"

They could see the flames leaping upward to the south of them. But Jay was already up the slope, slashing plants from their base and dragging them back to the truck. Suddenly, he howled in pain as a wasp nest on the ground erupted into fury. Lenny couldn't help laughing as his boss frantically pulled off his pants and ran from the stinging insects.

Moaning, he yelled to Lenny, "Bring those plants down!"

Keeping his head low, Lenny darted up the hill, grabbed the cut stalks, and took them down the hill to the truck. Jay had his pants back on now, and he joined Lenny in frantically jamming more and more plants into the truck.

"That's it," Jay said. "We just can't fit anymore."

Lenny handed him one of the bales of hay they had stacked on the ground, and Jay pushed it to the front of the load. He crawled out of the canopy door and together, they shoved another bale in the back of the truck. The canopy door wouldn't close completely. Jay fished in his pocket for a piece of twine and secured the partially open door to the bumper.

"Let's go," Jay said, sweating profusely from both the searing heat and the pain of the wasp stings.

Lenny was in the cab even before Jay. Neither one glanced back at Brutus. Jay turned the key in the ignition and listened as the engine sputtered and then died.

"What's the matter?" Lenny asked, looking panicky.

"The carburetor again," Jay muttered, trying again and again to start the engine. He jumped out of the truck and raised the hood. Lenny joined him. Even with the strong odor of smoke in the air, they both could smell the gasoline.

Lenny took the air filter off the carburetor. Gasoline was spilling over the top.

"It's flooded," Jay said angrily, smashing his fist against the side of the truck. "Here, I'll hold the choke open—you try to start it."

For several minutes, the men wrestled with the truck. Lenny kept cranking the ignition while Jay fiddled with the choke. The engine sputtered each time and died.

Lenny swore and leaned out the window to Jay.

"Let's get outta here. It's only about two miles back to the road—someone will pick us up there."

Jay looked at Lenny incredulously.

"Have you forgotten why we're here? You want to run? Okay, run, but I'm staying here, and when I get this truck started, I'm the sole owner of its contents."

Lenny looked at the ground sullenly.

"How long do you think it will take to get it started?"

"Dunno—I'm going to wait a half hour if I can and then try again—go cool your feet in the stream if you want," Jay said.

With an anxious eye on the sky, Lenny walked down to the stream. For the moment, it looked like the fire had stopped advancing, although it was so smoky, it was hard to tell. Lenny washed his face in the cool water and sat down on a rock. Thoughts of Mexico filtered through his brain again, and he looked back up the hill where Jay was bent over the engine.

* * * * * * * *

10 a.m. Vista Peak

Kim gave a small inward cheer as she watched the fire stop in its path and then reverse. A slight change in the wind was holding it at bay south of her, and for the moment, it looked like it might not come any farther up the canyon. Tankers and helicopters kept assaulting the fire's front line.

Like an ardent fan rooting for a football team, Kim mentally sent her encouragement to all those fighting the fire. *Push 'em back, push 'em back, way back,* was the refrain that kept going through her brain.

One lookout had already been evacuated, but for the moment, all the others were safe. Vista Peak was now the closest to the fire—approximately one and a half miles away.

* * * * * * * *

10:15 a.m.
Salem, Oregon

"Have you heard anymore?" Kim's mother said to her husband, who'd just hung up the phone.

"No, I can't even get through to the Ranger Station. Their phone lines are overloaded. I just called the U.S. Forest Service here in town. The person I talked to couldn't give me much information—just reassured me that lookouts are always evacuated if there's any danger."

"Yes, but they don't know our daughter. She's not one to run from anything. Oh, I just hope she doesn't do anything foolish," Mrs. Stafford said, wringing her hands.

"She left before when there was that lightning storm. Remember that? In fact, she didn't even try to save her Amateur Radio equipment. I think Kim's got a lot more sense than we give her credit for," Mr. Stafford said.

Mrs. Stafford brightened.

"You're right, dear. I know I shouldn't worry, but it's hard."

She walked over to the living room and looked out at the gray-black skies.

* * * * * * * *

For exactly twenty-two minutes, Incident Commander Bernaldi had seen a ray of hope. The winds had changed slightly bringing the advancing fire to a virtual standstill. But just as he was making plans to push the deadly enemy back onto its own charred territory, the wind changed again and breathed new life into the flames. With a crackling roar, it began to advance once again.

* * * * * * * *

10:20 a.m.

Jay tried the starter one more time.

"It's no use," Lenny protested. "Let's get out of here."

Jay ignored him. He grabbed a tool-chest from underneath the seat and opened it on the ground beside the open hood.

"What are you doing?" Lenny asked, as Jay grabbed a spark plug and pulled it out.

"They're all soaked with gas. That's why it won't start," Jay said grimly. "We're going to clean every one of them and put them back in."

"How long will that take?" Lenny was dancing nervously back and forth from foot to foot.

"I don't know," Jay said. "But however long it takes, we're gonna do it. It's our only chance. Here, wipe this one off."

* * * * * * * *

10:40 a.m.

"KA7SJP from KA7ITR."

There was a pause and then Kim's breathless voice. "KA7ITR from KA7SJP."

"Kim, they just let me through a few minutes ago with no guarantees of how far I'd get before they close the road. I'm within five miles of your trailhead though."

No answer.

"KA7SJP from KA7ITR"

"KA7SJP from KA7ITR. Kim?"

"Marc. The order just came over the radio to evacuate immediately. I've got to go. Since there's no helicopter landing site up here, they want to make sure I have time to get down the trail. If you can get to the trailhead, wait for me there."

"Roger, Kim. Be careful."

Marc called her several more times, but there was no answer. He looked at his odometer. Just one more mile. He drove around a long curve and groaned. There was a roadblock. Marc leaned out his window.

"Sorry, sir, the highway has just been closed. The fire is getting pretty near, and there are going to be air tanker drops in the vicinity. We can't risk anyone getting hurt."

"Listen," Marc protested. "My friend is a lookout at Vista Peak. I'm in radio contact with her, and she's just been evacuated. I told her I'd pick her up at the trailhead."

"I'm sorry, sir, but we can't allow you to go in there. Someone from the Forest Service will pick up your friend."

Marc realized the futility of protesting. He backed up and turned around. In his mind, he was trying to visualize the road that came up to the base of the trail that led to Kim's lookout. There was a logging road that intersected it from the east. Of that, he was sure. In fact, he and Kim had walked part way down it one day.

Marc pulled out a hiking map of the area he'd bought from a sporting goods store and studied it closely. He couldn't be sure, but there was a faint line less than a mile from Kim's trailhead. It looked like a road, and yes, it did intersect with the other road.

He wasn't an engineering student for nothing. The first rule he'd learned was that if one method didn't work, try another. Marc drove back around the curve out of view of the deputy manning the roadblock. Sure enough, on the right side of the road was a narrow road. An orange flag hung from the lower branch of a fir tree to the side. He shifted the truck into low and pushed down the gas pedal.

Chapter 19

Running

Friday, 10:42 a.m.
Vista Peak

I n ten minutes, the fire doubled its speed. As if wanting to make up for its brief pause, it burst forth with new energy, racing directly up the hill toward the lookout station. The two-meter hand-held radio was the only possession Kim had time to grab as she ran out the door.

The lookout station itself was on a small knoll above the tops of the trees flanking Vista Peak. The wave of fire cresting through trees could easily sweep over the lookout as the fire jumped from one source of fuel to the next. Gasping and coughing, Kim ran down the trail. Her last transmission received on the Forest Service radio promised her that someone would pick her up at the base of the trail. She hoped that Marc would be there too and that he could drive her to Detroit.

But first, Kim had to get to the bottom of the trail! The fire was a living, breathing beast behind her. Trying to fill her tortured lungs with air, she pounded down the path, slipping and sliding on rocks. An arm of the fire had already circled below her earlier in the morning but then retreated when the wind changed. Now the smoldering embers leaped into being again, and as Kim hurried around the bend at the base of her mountain, she stopped in horror. Two burning firs had fallen directly across the trail.

Desperately, she looked for a way around them. The dropoff to the left of the trail was too steep for her to climb. Only the brushy plateau to the right was open, and the fire was closing on that rapidly in both directions. *But the stream is just below that plateau*, Kim thought frantically as she beat her way through tall brush that tore her jeans. She had thrown off her sweatshirt as she ran, and her upper body protected by only a light shirt, was now badly scratched.

She felt as if she were trapped in a nightmare. Her brain signaled her legs to move and no matter how hard she tried, they wouldn't move fast enough. Shoving the thick bushes away with her hands, Kim fought her way across the field to the stream embankment. Berry vines at the top of the slope ripped her skin, but Kim didn't feel anything as she clambered down the rocky streambank to the welcome water below.

She waded directly into the water in her tennis shoes, letting the icy-cold water cool her burning feet and ankles. The smoke was less down in this small ravine, and Kim inhaled deeply. The fire had reached the tree tops that bordered the stream at the top of the hill. She knew it would be only minutes before its fury swept along this corridor. The stream was way too small to be a safe haven. One falling tree and she'd be dead.

Kim had to get moving, but even as her brain told her to leave, she remained motionless. Everything seemed frozen in time as she stood in the water, waiting for her pounding heart to slow to just double time. A doe and its fawn crashed through the underbrush into the stream. Kim jumped backward as the pair, mouths open and breathing hard, rushed past her up the stream. Startled, Kim watched them disappear. Should she follow them? Huge explosions down the hill told her that the fire had swept around behind her, and that she was caught in the pincers of its vise. The only way out was straight ahead. Kim thought frantically.

There was another trail on the other side of the stream. It was the one she often walked—the one where she had met the strange man one night. She had no idea where it led, but at the moment, it was out of the path of the fire. With renewed energy, Kim climbed the opposite embankment and jogged down the trail.

Automatically, she flipped on her two-meter rig in her pocket as she ran. She didn't have enough breath to talk, but maybe if she could just put a little distance between herself and the fire, she could get Marc to let the fire service know of her predicament.

He was already calling her.

"KA7SJP from KA7ITR."

Breathless, Kim dispensed with the formalities.

"Marc, where are you? Regular trail is blocked. I'm on one to the east of the Vista Creek Drainage—not sure where it goes—get a message to Dispatch for me."

She stopped talking to hold her sides and try to draw in more air.

"Hang in there, Kim. I'm on a road east of you too—I'm hoping it's going to run into your trail. Uh...got a slight problem. Looks like there's been some fire here, and there's a tree top across the road. Not too big though. I think I can move it with the truck. Just keep on running, Kim."

Gasping, Kim acknowledged his transmission. The tremendous exertion, heat, and lack of oxygen were making her feel light-headed. She stopped for a few seconds and then forced herself down the trail.

* * * * * * * *

Quickly, Marc switched his two-meter transceiver from simplex to a local repeater. He called for help and was immediately answered by a young woman amateur, Linda Peters, K6OQD, in the small town of Detroit, Oregon, nearby.

"Call the Ranger Station," Marc told her. "Tell them their Vista Peak lookout is caught east of her exit trail on the south fork of the Vista Creek Drainage. The fire has closed her off. I'm trying to get to her, but I'm not sure I'm even on the same road."

"Where are you?"

"On some sort of a logging road—there was an orange flag near the entrance—first road east of the Vista Peak trailhead."

Linda told Marc she would make the call immediately and then monitor for him continuously.

* * * * * * * *

Jeff Wilson, a U.S. Forest Service summer employee, glanced at his watch nervously. The young woman he had been sent to pick up should have been at the bottom of the trail five minutes ago. Flames were licking along the ridge directly above the trail. He radioed back to the Ranger Station. Did they want him to go up the trail looking for her?

"Negative," was the reply. A call had just come in from an Amateur Radio operator in Detroit saying Kim had been forced down another trail. They had a helicopter in the air now trying to figure out exactly where she was.

One of the fire officials spotted Jeff's car and stopped to shout to him.

"Move on out—this whole area's going to go up any minute."

"But..." Jeff protested.

The flames had crested the hill now and were racing down toward the road. Reluctantly, Jeff hurriedly turned his car around and headed back toward Detroit.

* * * * * * * *

Marc wrestled with the heavy tire chains. He fastened two of them together and looped his newly fashioned sling around the smaller end of the tree. Everything was coated with a red sticky goo—some sort of fire retardant, he guessed. Well, it had done its job. The wood still felt hot, but it wasn't burning.

He tied a rope to the chain harness and secured it to his truck's front bumper. He would have rather pulled the log from behind, but there was no way to turn the truck around in this small area. Praying silently that it would work, he put the truck in reverse and urged it backward. The engine immediately died. Marc started it again and revved the engine slowly before trying to start pulling. The rope tightened and he eased his vehicle backward.

The tree trunk moved only six inches before miring down in a deep rut. One of the branches was stuck in the ground, preventing the trunk from moving. Marc ran to his toolbox to get a small handsaw he always carried.

Sawing furiously, he worked on the branch until it gave way and he was able to drag it clear. He got back in the truck and started the pulling process once again.

* * * * * * * *

Friday 10:45 a.m.
Portland, Oregon

John Lawrence was delighted to hear from his old friend, Art Peterson, in Sisters, Oregon. They hadn't seen each other in five years.

"That son Marc of yours is a great guy," Art told John. "We're just so glad he spent the night."

"Spent the night?"

"Yeah, poor kid was sure disappointed about the fire and the music festival being shut down."

There was a short silence. Then John Lawrence, his voice tense with worry, starting asking questions.

"Look, Art, you'd better fill me in. My wife and I just got home from a week's trip to Missouri last night—visiting relatives. We'd heard something about a fire in Oregon but none of the specifics. I haven't seen a paper or turned on the radio. What's going on anyway?"

Art told him all about the Cascade fire that was now partially controlled south of Bend.

"But the one they're really worried about is the one up here southeast of Detroit Lake. That's partly why I called. Marc left here a couple of hours ago—said he was going to stop and see that girlfriend of his at the lookout. I'm sure he's just fine, but I just think I'd rest easier if you'll give me a call when he gets home tonight."

"Sure thing, Art," John said, a strange look on his face. "I'll do that."

Art seemed very chatty. Asked a lot of questions about their trip and various friends they had in common.

"Look, Art, can I call you back later. I think I need to make some phone calls and find out about that fire."

"Well sure, John, sorry if I've worried you. When Marc left, Highway 20 was open all the way. I haven't heard anything different since then."

* * * * * * * *

It took John Lawrence twenty minutes to get through to someone who could give him information about the Santiam Highway. He tried every possible line to the Forest Service and to both the Ranger Station at Sisters and Detroit. All were busy. Finally, he reached the Marion County Sheriff's Department and learned that the highway had just been closed.

"What is it dear?" his wife said, seeing the expression on his face as he hung up the phone.

"Probably nothing, probably nothing at all. But I'll sure feel better when we hear from Marc. You know, I think I'll call Kim's parents. Maybe they know something."

They didn't. All John Lawrence learned was that the Staffords were terribly worried. And from the Staffords' window, they had an excellent view of the enormous black clouds obscuring the mountains.

* * * * * * * *

"There," said Jay, putting the last spark plug back in. "If this doesn't do it, nothing will. Get in the cab, and turn it on."

Fearfully, Lenny cranked the engine, waiting to hear the reassuring noise of it catching hold. It started, then sputtered, and stopped.

"Stop a minute," Jay yelled. "Let me try holding the choke open again." He forced the choke open and held it with the screwdriver handle. "Start it, Lenny. I said, START IT!! What are you doing in there."

Jay turned to look at Lenny who was pointing a finger at the trail coming down the hill. A soot-streaked young woman with bleeding scratches on her arms was running right at them!

"What the?" Jay said. He put down his tools and turned to face this intruder.

* * * * * * * *

Sweat pouring down him, Marc pushed and shoved a branch under the end of the log until the end raised slightly. Now, maybe now, it could be dragged. He jumped back in his truck and slowly let the clutch out while depressing the gas pedal. The engine whined under its load, budged the log six inches forward, and then gave back three. Gently, Mark rocked the truck back and forth, trying to build up momentum with each tug. His back wheels spun, and he feared that he might be digging himself in.

There has to be a way, he thought. *Maybe the other end might move.* Quickly, he unfastened the chain harness and slid it around and under the opposite end of the broken tree-top. After tightening the rope, he got in the truck and urged the truck forward. The log was moving! To be sure, just inches at a time, but it was moving.

Fearing he might snap the rope or the chains under the tremendous strain, Marc eased the truck forward until the rope was taut and once again coaxed the log forward a few more inches. He looked at the heavy brush on both sides of the road. Even as sturdy as his truck was, it couldn't drive through that. He would have to get the log turned halfway to get through. And where was Kim? Supposing he were doing all this, and she was running down some other road?

With one hand on the wheel, he grabbed his radio and called her.

"Kim? Where are you, Kim?"

Chapter 20

"Easy, Brutus...Easy"

Friday, noon.

As soon as K6OQD in Detroit relayed Marc's distress call, the grim information went out to fire and law enforcement units that both a lookout and another person were trapped behind the fire perimeter. Weary line fighters led by equally exhausted fire officials pondered their next action. Never had anyone experienced an Oregon blaze with this much energy. Since the fire had begun on United States forest land, the person in charge of all the personnel battling the blaze was U.S. Forest Service Incident Commander Leo Bernaldi, also called the "fire boss." A 58-year old man, with an illustrious military service background of infantry command in both Korea and Vietnam, Bernaldi saw the Santiam Fire as difficult an enemy as any he had ever faced.

The fire seemed to have a thinking brain of its own. Now, it was using the fire fighters' own tactics: circle and contain. Its searing clutches had almost completed a deathly sphere— a two-mile oblong with a half-mile radius at its narrowest point. That precious fire-free zone contained the lives of Kim, Marc, Jay, Lenny, and Brutus.

Pointing to a detailed map, Bernaldi told one of his crew leaders, "The lookout and her friend may be up that road, but we can't get to them. It's blocked. Fire's pouring down that chute off the ridge right now with unbelievable speed. I can't possibly put a unit in there—best we can do is order some tanker drops on the perimeter." He shook his head sadly.

"And we don't even know for sure where these people are. None of the aerial units has spotted anyone. We're alerting everyone in the air now, but I'm not hopeful anyone can be seen through this smoke."

Bernaldi turned to listen for new information coming in over his radio. They had set up a fire camp in the state park across from the Ranger Station, so that they would have easy access to water and phone lines. The park was full of off-duty fire fighters—eating, sleeping, or getting ready for their next duty shift. A couple of them drifted over to listen to what their "I.C." (Incident Commander) had to say.

For the moment, the fire seemed intent on widening its circle, rather than filling in the hollow in its center. But Commander Bernaldi knew that soon, it would sense its unused fuel, and there would be no hope for anyone caught in its grip.

"We've got additional help coming, but right now I'm sending the ones I do have to the edge of that road to see if we can't find a way in," Bernaldi said, watching the fiery sky. "If those two people are in there, we've got to try to establish an escape route."

* * * * * * * *

Run! Run! Kim's brain told her.

Can't do it, Can't do it, her tortured lungs and legs answered.

Yes, you can! was her brain's answering command.

Kim forced her smoke-stung eyes open as she pounded down the trail into a small clearing. A truck! Two men! She couldn't believe what she was seeing. With relief, she ran to them.

"Help me," she gasped, almost staggering to the ground. Then she stopped, mouth open in terror. One of the men had a gun pointed at her.

"No! Don't do that!" Kim pleaded. "The fire's coming. Whoever you are, please take me out of here."

She collapsed to her knees, half sobbing with exhaustion and fear. There was the sound of the truck engine starting and an exhilarated shout from the other man.

"I got it," Lenny yelled. "Come on, let's go—you gonna take her along or what?"

"Keep it going," Jay said smiling. "No, I'm not going to take this young lady with us." He walked over toward Kim, appraising her, while she watched helplessly. "But I am going to leave her some company."

Jay ran over to Brutus and quickly unchained him. The dog tried to follow Jay as he ran to the truck, but he ordered the starving dog back. With a gesture of his arm toward Kim, Jay yelled "Brutus, Guard!" In a flash, Jay was back in the truck and the two men with their load of green gold were rocketing down the road.

"Stop!" Kim yelled. "Don't leave..."

Desperately, Kim stumbled after the truck but then stopped as the tawny, savage-looking dog came running toward her. The animal stopped three feet in front of Kim, freezing her with his direct gaze and his body stiff at attention. Every muscle in his body was poised for attack and Kim could hear the nervous clicking of his teeth. Saliva dripped from his open, panting mouth.

* * * * * * *

Salem—Stafford's home

"News of the expected containment of the Cascade Inferno blaze has been considerably lessened by reports that the Santiam Fire is burning out of control. An unusually dry spring and summer coupled with unseasonably hot August temperatures has made Oregon's forest areas especially vulnerable to fire. One official we spoke with earlier this morning said he had never seen a blaze with as much energy as the Santiam Fire. Easterly winds continue to spread the fire into new areas. The fire has turned north and is now threatening communities along Highway 22. The town of Idanha has been evacuated, and all roads into the area are closed. This has been a special news bulletin."

Mrs. Stafford turned off the radio.

"Why doesn't she call? Kim knows how we worry about her."

"Try not to worry, dear," Mr. Stafford said, putting his arm around his wife. "She may not be able to get to a phone or it may be that all the lines are busy. You know, we've been trying to call the Ranger Station and can't get through."

"Well, why doesn't she use that Amateur Radio of hers? She's certainly gotten messages to us that way before."

"I'm sure we'll hear soon. Just try to be patient," Mr. Stafford said, but he didn't sound convinced himself.

* * * * * * * *

Commander Bernaldi held the two-way radio to his ear. It was hard to hear over the roar of the fire and sirens. He had just called in coordinates for a slurry drop on the edge of the fire near the road east of the lookout. First, he moved his units out of the way. The retardant would hit the ground with such force that it was imperative that everyone be out of the way.

As soon as he saw Air Tanker 67 drop its red liquid load, he called the fire fighters back in. Hopefully, the slurry would cool down the area enough that they could open up the road a little more. But if the wind should start pushing the fire directly at them, he would have to call them back.

* * * * * * * *

A foot! This time the log had moved a whole foot. Then his truck engine died. It was a delicate seesaw balance keeping the clutch and the gas pedal in exactly the right proportion to allow the engine to pull such a heavy load. Marc started the truck once again and slowly let out the clutch. The truck strained, and the engine whined, but the log moved forward another six inches. He started the truck once again, but the fallen tree refused to budge.

Marc got out of the truck and ran to the log. Maybe, just maybe, he could squeeze his truck through the space he had created. He looped the rope around his front bumper but left the chain harness over the log. There wasn't time to get such unimportant things now.

The tree branches scraped the side of his truck on the right and the heavy brush buffeted it on the left, but Marc managed to get the truck through an inch at a time. He rolled up the truck windows, hoping to keep out the searing heat from the fire.

"Kim?" he shouted into his two-meter rig. No answer. Briefly, as he bounced down the rutted road toward the fire, he wondered if he was driving into his own death.

* * * * * * * *

With a sob, Kim sat down, dazed by the events of the last few minutes. The dog was a Pit Bull, of that she was fairly certain. And those horrible men who had left her to die in the fire had given him some sort of command to watch her. Kim coughed softly and wiped her eyes with her hand. The dog, watching every gesture, moved a few inches closer.

Suddenly, Kim was no longer afraid. In fact, she felt a peaceful calm as she rationally assessed her situation. The fire was moving toward them. The heat was so intense that she felt a strange prickling sensation on her skin. And here she was guarded by a dog, whose fierceness made the newspapers almost every day.

Kim turned her head slightly to look over at the road down which the two men in the truck had disappeared. The road was shrouded in smoke, but it offered her only hope. Inch by inch, Kim started to ease into a standing position. The dog moved another step closer and curled its lip menacingly.

His eyes were bloodshot and occasionally, the dog lifted a front paw to rub against his burning eyes. As Kim half crouched, barely breathing, she could see raw bleeding spots where the chain collar had dug into his neck from his frantic attempts to free himself.

"You poor thing," she said soothingly. "Brutus? Is that your name?"

The dog looked at her and cocked his head slightly. He didn't move as Kim straightened into a standing position. His thoughts were a mixture of torment from the smoke and hunger. The men who usually brought food and water had left him again.

In a wolf pack, the Alpha leader had total control over his underlings. Brutus had accepted Jay as his leader, the Alpha or "top dog." He would do his bidding in the faithful way that dog has always carried out man's wishes.

But now his leader was gone. His leader no longer fed him. Here was a young woman who despite her strong smell of smoke triggered an ancient memory in his brain. It was a very pleasant memory.

"Brutus, easy Brutus."

Kim reached her left hand into her pocket for her radio, but then suddenly withdrew it and plunged her right hand into her other pocket. Brutus jerked at the sudden movement and stared intensely at Kim. Purposefully, she avoided his eye contact. She didn't want to do anything that would invite confrontation.

Kim had never had a bad experience with any dog, but common sense told her that Brutus meant business. She would have to move cautiously.

"Sorry, Brutus, old boy. Didn't mean to put my hand in my pocket so fast. You're a good dog, Brutus." She used his name over and over, coupled with "good dog" and "boy," hoping desperately that some of the words had friendly associations in his mind.

Now her fingers had hold of some small pieces of beef jerky in her right pocket. Marc had bought it for her at the Saturday market in Portland, and she'd been nibbling on it occasionally during her evening walks. Ever so slowly, she pulled her hand out and tossed the jerky halfway between her and Brutus. She knew it was a risky move. The smell of food might trigger the dog into attacking.

Brutus hesitated only a second before snatching the seasoned piece of meat. Kim watched him as he wolfed it down and then looked at her expectantly for more. She knelt and held the remaining pieces in her open hand. Watching her carefully, the dog walked stiff-legged toward her. His nose twitched, and Kim heard a strange whine come from his throat. Then the dog was carefully eating the meat from her hand. She sat still, with her empty hand out to him. Hesitantly, he reached forward and sniffed it. His warm tongue licked her palm.

"Oh, Brutus," Kim said gratefully. "You poor thing. Come on, boy, let's get out of here."

She got up cautiously. Brutus didn't move. Kim walked slowly toward the road. Brutus stood, watching her, and then almost meekly, trotted behind her. Kim kept talking to him, urging him to follow.

"Come on, Brutus, good boy, good Brutus. Let's go, Brutus."

She dared not run, but when the dog offered no hostility, Kim eased into a trot. Soon, she was running down the road, the dog following just a few feet behind.

"Marc," she spoke urgently into her microphone. "Marc? I'm on a road somewhere—oh, please hear me Marc!"

Chapter 21

Man's Best Friend

Friday, 12:30 p.m.

"**W**e shoulda taken her with us, boss," Lenny complained as they bounced along the logging road.

"You always got a thing for a pretty girl, don't you?" Jay laughed, in spite of the smoke that was making them both cough. "And I could tell she was pretty—even under all that soot and dirt. But let me tell you something—that was one pretty girl that meant big trouble. What would we do with her? Let her out on the highway? You don't think she'd have questions about what we were doing in here?"

"Wouldn't have had to tell her nothing," Lenny still protested.

"Yeah, well maybe not. But what happens when the cops start asking her how she got out and stuff, and then she tells them about us...and if she thinks real hard, she maybe remembers what we look like and maybe even our license plate. How 'bout that Lenny?"

"Guess you're right. Just seems too bad. So young and so pretty. You s'pose Brutus chewed her up pretty good?"

Jay looked in the rearview mirror. Columns of fire were rocketing skyward behind them in the vicinity of their marijuana field. They had literally gotten out minutes ahead of the fire.

"I doubt it matters much, Lenny. Let's just think about getting out of here and getting this stuff sold. Hey, Lenny, we're going to be rich—not as rich as we hoped, but rich!" Jay reached over and slapped Lenny on the back.

* * * * * * *

Marc turned on his windshield wipers to clear away some of the falling ash. He knew better than to push the squirter button. Liquid would turn what visibility he had into mud. Occasionally, a shower of embers danced across the hood of his truck.

"Marc? Where are you, Marc?"

"KA7SJP—Kim!! Where are you?"

"Running," was her gasping reply. "I'm running down some road."

"I'm on a road too—your signal's really loud. I bet I'm coming right at you!"

"Marc, there are some men," ... she paused to catch her breath ... "they're armed ... in a brown truck ... be careful."

Kim said something else, but she was breathing so hard, Marc couldn't make it out. He didn't have time to ask her to repeat. A large brown form was moving at him out of the smoke cloud ahead.

"We must be on the same road, Kim. Here come your friends..."

"Marc! Listen, Marc!"

Marc's two-meter radio plummeted to the floor, as he slammed on the brakes and hit the horn with his fist in an effort to warn the other truck. He skidded sideways, the tail end of the truck stuck in the tall brush at the roadside. Shaking, he waited.

* * * * * * * *

Jay's eyes opened wide in alarm as the blue truck blocking the road ahead of them became visible. He laid on the horn, but even as he did, it was obvious there was no place for the other vehicle to move on the barely eight-foot-wide road.

"Go around him!" Lenny shouted.

"Can't," Jay said, braking to a stop. "Brush is too high—we'd get stuck."

Jay reached under the seat for his pistol. Marc was already out of his truck, walking toward him. He stopped a few feet away from the cab, looking hesitantly at the men. Jay leaned out the window, the loaded gun hidden under his shirt on the seat beside him.

"Back your truck up!" he barked.

"I was going to ask you to do the same thing," Marc said evenly. "There's a girl trapped by the fire back there. I've got to get to her."

"Not much left to get to by now," Lenny snorted. He giggled and poked Jay to see if he had appreciated his humor, but Jay ignored him.

Jay opened the door, keeping the pistol beside him, out of view, behind the door. With a quick motion, he brought it up, aimed at Marc.

"Move that truck! Now!"

* * * * * * * *

Incident Commander Bernaldi was on the phone with Linda Peters, K6OQD, the Amateur Radio operator who had relayed Marc's distress call.

"Have you heard any more from the young man?"

"Yes, but not directly," Linda said. "I was just going to call you. He originally contacted me on a local repeater. I've been calling him on that frequency but there's been no answer. So I started monitoring simplex, and just a minute ago, I heard him talking to a young woman. Sort of talking, that is. She was out of breath. Was trying to warn him about some men in a truck. He went back to her once and now they're both off the air. I've been trying to call them both—they're not using call letters … Kim and Marc, I think their names are—but there's no answer."

Bernaldi scratched his head. Men in a truck? What was going on here?

"Tell me again where he said his location was, the first time you talked to him," he asked her.

"He said the first road east of the lookout trailhead. Said there was an orange flag on a tree by the road. Said she was east of the Vista Drainage."

"There are three roads right close together, and there are flags on all of them—in fact half the roads around here are flagged—markers for the logging trucks," Bernaldi told her. "If he was coming from the east, I'm wondering how he knew it was the road closest to the lookout. Actually, he's wrong, now that I think about it. The highway department was stopping traffic in between the second and third road, so there's no way he went down the road next to the lookout. So the question is, did he go down the first or the second road?"

"If he was looking at a map, what road would he think he was on?" asked Linda.

"Doesn't show any on a regular Oregon map, but if he had something like this district map I've got here, it only shows one road—the one closest to the lookout. Those other two were put in last year by one of the logging companies. Sure wish we knew for sure which one he's on," Bernaldi said thinking aloud.

"He must be trying to rescue the lookout," Linda said "I'm sure of that—someone here who knows Kim pretty well said she has a boyfriend."

The incident commander told Linda good-bye and asked her to contact him immediately with any new information. Looking around, he called one of the fire crew leaders over.

"Latest estimate from the air is that the open area is one third of a mile by one and a half miles. But there are several spots where the fire is burning directly across the open area. The lead plane reported several small fires in the center of the circle—the whole thing could torch any time."

The crew leader listened somberly to this latest information.

"You still want us to try to get in on one of those roads? Which one?" he asked.

The two possible roads had been designated E1 and E2—E2 being the closest to Kim's lookout.

"I guess...well, let's hope the young man somehow knew about both roads. Let's take him literally and try to break through to E2. I just hope that's the right choice," Bernaldi said.

"Right now, I'm calling in a chopper to take me up for a look see. I doubt I can see anything the tankers can't, but I at least want to give it a try."

Bernaldi told his radio operator to get a message to Dispatch at Redmond Air Center. Both tankers were in the process of being refueled and reloaded with retardant, but they would be air ready in just a few minutes. Bernaldi told them he would shortly be talking to them directly from the air.

He sighed after he ended his transmission to the Air Tanker Dispatch. The force of the fire made the air alive with heat and energy. He feared that it wouldn't be long until he had to order all of his line units to retreat. As he glanced toward the smoke-obscured mountains, he knew the Santiam Fire was winning.

* * * * * * * *

E2 was exactly one quarter of a mile west of the road where two trucks and three men were facing an impasse. If the humans had looked skyward, they might have seen or heard, the huge air tankers flying in to drop loads of slurry. But their attention was focused on each other. Focused on each other and their vehicles which blocked them from reaching their goals.

"Back it up!" Jay said harshly as he walked toward Marc, menacing him with the gun.

"Look at my truck!" Marc shouted. "It's stuck the way it is—the only way I can move it is if you back up and let me try and bring it forward."

Jay was in no mood to be logical. He jammed the pistol into Marc's ribs.

"Back his truck up, Lenny."

Lenny ran obediently to the truck and tried to get it to go backwards. Marc's prediction was right. The truck wouldn't budge. The squeal of spinning tires and the rear of the truck bouncing against brush filled the air.

"Okay, get out!" Jay yelled to Lenny. "That was a stupid idea anyway. No telling how far we'd have to back his to find a clear spot. Let's tip this baby on its side. Come on, help me."

Without questioning, Lenny walked around to join Jay at the side of Marc's truck. Anxiously, Marc watched the men struggle to tip the two-ton pickup. But then he relaxed as he realized that even with the back end slightly askew in the brush, there was no way they were going to be able to topple that much weight.

He could run—they weren't watching him. His brain considered that possibility and quickly rejected it. The flames were closing in rapidly on all sides. If there were any way to get to Kim and then out of here, he knew they would need the speed of a vehicle.

"Listen," he said to the straining men. "I don't know who you are and I don't care. You want to go out and I want to go in. There's only one way for us to get these trucks moving and that's for you to back up and let me go forward until we find a clear spot where we can pass each other." In a rage, Jay let go of the truck frame. His legs burned and ached from the multiple wasp stings. Never known for his patience, his anger reached the boiling point. They had almost been home free and now here was this college-sounding kid telling him what to do.

"Lenny, pull our truck up to his bumper. We're gonna ram him off the road."

"No!" Marc protested, grabbing at Lenny's arm as he started toward his truck.

"Let go of me, you punk kid," Lenny said, trying to shake Marc off, but the young man hung on doggedly.

Jay was almost relieved to finally have a target on which to focus his anger. He pulled the gun out of his waistband where he had tucked it.

"Stop!" yelled a hoarse female voice. Jay's head jerked up. The girl! The girl, who should be dead by now, was running right at them! Reflexively, Jay turned to aim at this new target. His arm never had a chance to be fully extended.

Marc's booted foot hit his gun hand with such force that the pistol went flying.

Howling with pain and rage, Jay turned to tackle Marc. Always ready for a good fight, Lenny jumped into the fracas and started pummeling Marc.

Soon there was a new combatant added to the fray. Drawing on her last reserves of energy, Kim raced the last few yards and desperately tried to pull the two big men off Marc. One of them lashed backwards with his hand at this pesky interference and Kim went flying backwards.

That was all it took for Brutus. He had been standing, panting, watching this noisy human squabble. Even though he knew the male participants, its outcome held no interest for him. All of his thoughts were centered on his own starving, heat and smoke tortured body.

But then something happened. One of the men hit the girl. The girl who had fed him some delicious pieces of meat and spoken softly to him. He heard her cry out as she hit the ground a few feet away from the fight. Silently, his magnificently muscled body flew into the air. With deadly accuracy, his powerful jaws grabbed Jay's right arm. His teeth closed, crunching through the bones of his forearm.

The ensuing scream stopped the fight. Never had Lenny or Marc heard such a sound as the bloodcurdling sound of pain coming from Jay's mouth.

"No...no...Brutus..." Jay screamed.

Lenny's eyes opened wide with terror. Then his brain chose what had seemed a logical option to him all along. He turned and ran down the road back toward the main highway.

Sickened by the blood coming from Jay's arm and his screams, Kim shouted to Brutus to stop. Amazingly, the dog loosened his grip and stood panting in front of Jay. With a backward glance, Jay saw Lenny's retreating form. He looked down at Brutus, whose open mouth was flecked with blood, and at Marc who had retrieved the gun from the bushes and now had it aimed at him.

Sobbing and holding his injured arm, he turned and ran after his partner.

Chapter 22

In a Closing Circle

Friday 1 p.m.

Kim and Marc stood motionless, staring at each other. Brutus, who had given brief chase to Jay and Lenny, was now standing between them, breathing heavily.

"You okay?" Marc asked quietly, moving over to put his arm around her.

Brutus took a step toward Marc as if to protect Kim.

"It's okay, Brutus. Easy, boy. Good dog," she reassured him.

Brutus sat down on his haunches, eyeing Marc warily.

One whole side of Kim's face was red where Jay had hit her. She looked up at Marc. The corner of his mouth was bleeding and his left eye was rapidly swelling shut.

"Better than you, I think," she said, half-smiling. "Come on, let's get out of here."

"That may be easier said than done," Marc said. "Here, get in their truck and back it up. The only way out of that brush is straight forward."

"Wait a minute, Marc. There's someone who's going with us."

She snapped her fingers and called to Brutus gently as she went around to the back of Marc's truck.

"You have room for him in there?" she asked.

"You bet."

Marc lifted the canopy and shoved his bass over to one side.

"Will he let me lift him in?" Marc asked.

"I wouldn't try it," Kim cautioned.

She patted her hand on the open tail gate and called to Brutus. Cautiously, he approached the truck. Truck rides had not exactly led to pleasant endings for him before. But this girl...her voice was soothing, and he trusted her. The dark haven of the canopy enclosure looked inviting. He coiled his muscles and leaped into the truck, skidding forward on the smooth surface.

"Good Brutus, good boy. You just sit down there. Good dog, Brutus."

Quickly, Kim shut the canopy door on Marc's truck and then ran over to the one belonging to Jay and Lenny. She fiddled with the gears for a minute and then slowly backed it down the road toward the fire she had just fled.

Marc revved his engine and the truck pulled forward, straining to free itself from the brush. He tried unsuccessfully several times and then waved to Kim to come back.

"You're going to have to pull me," he said.

Quickly, Marc unwrapped the rope from the front bumper where it was still tied. He fastened it to the front bumper of Jay and Lenny's truck, and just as Marc had done with the fallen tree, Kim now proceeded to pull Marc's truck. One steady pull and he was free. Marc unfastened the rope, and they were on their way.

Foot by foot, one truck going backwards and the other forward, they crept down the road. Marc saw the wide spot first. He honked and pointed. Kim backed beyond the spot, and Marc swung his truck into it.

There still wasn't much room for maneuvering, but Marc finally managed to get his truck turned around. Happily, Kim abandoned the other vehicle and ran to join him.

"Hang on," Marc said. "I'm going to try to get us out of here as fast as possible."

* * * * * * * *

"Stop!" Jay yelled to Lenny. "I just can't run any more," he moaned, sinking to the ground, cradling his injured arm. Lenny stood next to him, nervously eyeing the fire approaching from all sides. They had left the road twenty feet earlier because it was blocked by flame. The road dipped at that point, forming a natural draw and fire was sweeping through this narrow east-west avenue like a chimney. There didn't appear to be any way through.

"Come on," Lenny had insisted to Jay. "Go to the left—maybe there's an open area down there."

In pain, Jay had tried to keep up. In just a few quick moments, he and Lenny had reversed roles. They half-trotted at least a quarter of a mile, Lenny leading and Jay trying to follow. In truth, Jay wasn't sure what was the use of trying to outrun the fire. Everything he valued had been lost when they abandoned the truck.

Lenny saw it differently. His brain was still acting on the survival principle. If there was a chance of getting out of this inferno alive, he was going to seize that chance.

"Get up!" he ordered Jay.

Jay rose to his feet clumsily and staggered after Lenny. But there was no keeping up with him. Jay's arm was bleeding heavily. Combined with the intense heat and smoke from the fire, he was feeling faint. Very faint. He sank to the ground. Lenny looked over at him just once and then sprinted down the perimeter of the fire looking for an escape hole.

There! A hundred yards away where the draw rose and evened with the rest of the terrain, the width of the blaze narrowed from a hundred feet to just a few. Lenny ran breathlessly up to this point. He could actually see through the wall of flame to the forest on the other side.

Frantically, he scooped up handfuls of soil and threw them into the fire, but it was no use. The fire had too much fuel to be dampened by one man's puny efforts. Lenny looked desperately to the left. The fire was wider there. Taking a deep gasp of air, he pulled his shirt up over his face and ran headlong through the fire.

Lenny hit the ground on the other side like a baseball player reaching home plate. His clothes were on fire, and he rolled back and forth on the ground, extinguishing the flames. When he opened his eyes, he found to his amazement that he was alive. True, the skin on his arms looked very peculiar, and he felt a weird numbness in his entire body, but he was alive!

With a super-human effort, he got up and forced himself toward the barely visible highway in the distance. Fifty yards from his goal, he collapsed on the ground and, in shock, lapsed into unconsciousness.

* * * * * * *

Within seconds of the fire crew finding Lenny, U.S. Forest Service Incident Commander Leo Bernaldi was called to the scene. He radioed his Dispatcher at the Ranger Station and asked her to tell the helicopter to wait for him. He arrived at the place where Lenny had been found just as the burned man was being loaded into the ambulance.

"Where was he?" Bernaldi asked.

"Over there, about fifty yards from E2," one of the fighters replied, pointing.

Lenny was moaning and stirring, almost conscious. He opened his eyes briefly and looked at Bernaldi.

"Was there anyone else in there with you?" Bernaldi asked him.

Lenny eyes focused on the commander's face. He opened his mouth and spoke one word clearly.

"No," Lenny said.

* * * * * * *

"Let's see if the woman I talked to earlier is still there," Marc said, punching up the repeater frequency. "K6OQD from KA7ITR," as they jolted down the forestry road designated as E1.

Her relieved-sounding voice came back to him. "KA7ITR from K6OQD. Where are you, Marc? Do you have Kim with you?"

It didn't even dawn on Marc that he had never told this woman his name. Or to ask how she knew about Kim.

"Yes," he told her. "We're both together and we're driving down an access road to the highway. I think we're about a mile away from the junction."

"Marc, there's a fire at the edge of that road, but the fire crews are trying to clear access to you right now."

"Roger," Marc said, as he reached out to grab Kim's hand reassuringly.

* * * * * * *

Linda phoned the Ranger Station. Bernaldi was just walking out the door when the Dispatch Operator called to him. He picked up the phone.

"I'm talking to Marc," Linda said excitedly. "He and Kim are together driving out on an access road."

"Ask him if they encountered a man," Chief Bernaldi said. "Most of his hair is burned off, but he looks to be blond— about six feet tall."

"Stand by."

In a few seconds, Linda was back.

" 'You'd better believe it,' are Marc's exact words," Linda said.

"Okay, stay with him and stay on the phone here to relay to the Dispatcher," Bernaldi told her. "I think we know where they are. I'm going to be in the air, but anything you find out can be relayed to me."

Quickly, he contacted the Redmond Air Center. The victim they had just found was close to the mouth of road E2. Even though he denied there was anyone else in there, Marc's statement proved him a liar. Believing that since the injured man had been found near E2 that the others must be there too, Bernaldi asked the air tankers to hit the area around E2 with everything they had.

"We just got a relay message from one of the trapped parties through an Amateur Radio operator. We've got to clear a path for them," Bernaldi told the Air Tanker Dispatch. "I'm going up too, so I'll be talking to the pilots in case there's any change."

He expected no reply to his orders, but a minute later the dispatcher came back with an unusual request.

"Tell your Amateur Radio operators to change frequency to 146.52. I say again, 146.52."

"Roger," said Bernaldi.

* * * * * * * *

One of the crew bosses was calling Bernaldi on another Forest Service transmission frequency. As he ran across to the field to the waiting helicopter, he raised his hand-held radio to his ear and listened to the crew boss. The message was short. The fire had closed its circle. There were no longer any open escape routes at all. If anyone were to get in or out, the line of fire would have to be penetrated.

* * * * * * * *

"Oh no!" Kim cried out.

They had been shielded from a full view of the fire by winding road and stands of yet-unburnt timber. Now, as they rounded a curve, they saw the wall of fire engulfing the road. While there wasn't combustible material on the road itself, the leaps of flame from tree to tree across the narrow eight foot road made the fire an impenetrable entity.

"Linda!" Marc said desperately into his microphone. "Linda, tell them the road is blocked by fire!"

Linda forced herself to speak calmly.

"Marc, go to 146.52. Understand? 146.52."

Chapter 23

"The Drop"

"**R**eady to go back to the party?" Sil Myers, pilot of the giant C130 asked copilot Lance Rettig as they taxied down the runway at Redmond.

Lance nodded, but he was too busy to think of a clever comeback to his senior officer and good friend, Sil Myers. Lance was absorbed with hooking up his two-meter radio and attaching it to the short antenna against the window directly below his right leg.

Ordinarily when the Dispatch Operator gave them flying orders, it was all impersonal facts: coordinates, type of drop, amount to be released, etc. But Betty, their Dispatcher, had just radioed Lance with a special bit of information. The people stuck in the fire below were both Amateur Radio operators and were in contact with another operator in the small town of Detroit, twenty miles west of the fire.

There wasn't anyone associated with the Air Tanker Station who didn't know about Lance's involvement in Amateur Radio. Parked in the employee lot, his car, with its license plate KB7NLD, and multiple antennas, was a daily advertisement for the hobby. Betty felt he'd want to know that the trapped people were Amateur Radio operators, and she was right. It took Lance only a second to reply to Betty.

"Tell them to move to 146.52," he said.

Sil looked over at him, his eyebrows arched in question.

"Maybe, this will help," Lance said, tapping his two-meter rig.

* * * * * * * *

Kim and Marc anxiously watched the flames closing in on them from all sides. There was no escape. Behind them, ahead of them, to the left and right—four walls of fire eating away at the small fire-free zone on which their truck stood.

The heat was searing. In an attempt to keep some of the smoke out, Kim and Marc had rolled up the windows. They were sweating profusely and choking on the thick, hot air. The truck rocked back and forth as Brutus paced in the back. They could hear his whimpering and coughing. "We're going to die," Kim said softly.

"No, we're not!" Marc said back to her, fiercely, yet barely audible over the crackling explosions all around them. "I'm going to drive through that."

Kim's eyes opened wide with terror.

"But we can't see through it! We'll be burned alive! Wait just a few more seconds. Maybe a tanker will drop a load and clear the way."

The roar of the fire was so loud, Marc couldn't hear all that she said. But he nodded at "a few more seconds."

"Just a few," he said, positioning his foot on the gas pedal to accelerate.

A voice broke their tense wait.

"KA7ITR, this is KB7NLD from airborne Tanker 67, can you read me?"

"Yes," Marc said, grabbing the mike with shaking hands.

"Good. We can't see you two, but we believe you're right behind the fire on logging road E2. Are you in a vehicle?"

"Yes, ready to go," Marc said.

"Okay. Listen, we're going to drop retardant right ahead of you. Get your windshield wipers going and as soon as the stuff stops coming down, move yourselves out of there."

"Yes, sir," Marc said gratefully, reaching out to grab Kim's hand.

* * * * * * * *

"Can you see them?" Captain Sil Myers asked Incident Commander Leo Bernaldi.

"No," Bernaldi answered, as the pilot of the helicopter maneuvered his aircraft once again through the smoky area.

"We're going to drop across the road though and pray that's where they are."

"Roger," Sil told him.

Lance Rettig readied the drop. Due to the possibility that it might strike the vehicle of the trapped parties, they were going to do a "level four" coverage of 1500 gallons of slurry. A "level four" would hit the ground with considerably less force than their maximum "level six" which was 3000 gallons dumped in 1.5 seconds. Hopefully, the level four would be enough to do the job.

Lance took a quick look out the window as they banked and came around for the drop. Flame was shooting from the treetops and burning embers danced off the plane's windows like fireflies. He set the controls to open the huge bottom doors of the slurry tank and put his hand on the red button on the yoke, ready to deliver the load.

"Now," said Sil. "Now!"

But Lance removed his hand from the red button. As Sil turned to look at him in surprise, Lance tapped his finger against his earphone. Sil had been so intent on the drop, that for a second or two he didn't hear the hoarse male voice speaking to them.

"No!" Marc was telling them. "I just saw your plane and you're to the west of us. We're a quarter of a mile east of you!"

As the two-meter transmission was coming only into the C130, Lance quickly relayed the information to Bernaldi so he would know why they hadn't made the drop. Without hesitation, Bernaldi replied.

"We guessed wrong. They're on E1! Drop it there!"

* * * * * * * *

It doesn't take long to move a C130 a quarter of a mile, and this time Lance didn't pull his hand back from the red button. But before he depressed it, he transmitted to Marc for a final check.

"Are we above you?"

"Yes! Yes, I hear you!"

"Go for it kids!"

The slurry pounded down from the sky in an east-west pattern as Tanker 67 cooled down an entire quarter mile of flame that blazed in the shallow gulley that separated Marc and Kim from safety.

The edge of the drop hit their hood and the noise sounded like an ocean wave breaking right on top of them. The windows were completely coated with thick red liquid. Even after he turned on the wipers, Marc could barely see at all. He waited until the pounding noise stopped and then pushed down the gas pedal, let out the clutch, and floored it. Thick steam from the road poured in through the vents and filled the cab. Holding her breath, Kim clutched Marc's arm as they drove blindly through the swirling red.

"Marc! Marc! Are you okay?"

It was Lance Rettig's voice, but Marc didn't hear him. With a death grip on the steering wheel, and his eyes nearly shut against the searing steam and smoke, he pushed even harder on the gas pedal. The engine screamed, demanding to be shifted to a higher gear.

Like a rocket, Marc's truck launched over the potholes in the road and roared out of the fire.

"I see them!" Commander Bernaldi yelled into the mike on his headset. "They're clear!"

Sil Myers smiled as he banked the huge plane around to return to the Redmond Air Base.

"Sil, what's that saying you have?" Lance asked him. "Don't worry about anything because nothing will ever be all right?"

Sil laughed aloud.

"You know, I think I just saw something that may be all right."

* * * * * * * *

"We're out!" Kim shouted.

The wipers had cleared a tiny slot on her side of the window while Marc's was still completely covered with slurry.

Quickly, they both rolled down their windows and put their heads out to see where they were going. They were still in black smoke, but there were no flames here. Marc shifted into third and guided his truck through the unburnt trees to safety.

The fire crew that had been ready to invade the "cooled zone" once the tanker made its drop, stopped with their shovels resting on their shoulders as the blue truck shot by them toward Highway 22. Hastily, they followed the vehicle. The fire would regain its lost territory quickly.

"Are you okay?" a fire fighter shouted to Marc as they reached the road.

Marc nodded yes.

"Then follow that truck—this whole area's going to go up any minute."

The windshield wipers had cleared a considerable space now, and Kim and Marc watched as fire fighters piled onto the flatbed truck ahead of them. Too exhausted to say anything, they followed the truck a mile down the road until it stopped in a clearing.

The crew leader came back, this time to Kim's side.

"Our base camp is 15 miles down the road. You kids sure you're okay? One of us can drive for you, if you want?"

Kim looked over at Marc's smoke and sweat stained face and smiled.

"No," she said. "We're fine." As the crew leader returned to his truck, she said it again, this time to Marc. "We're fine. We're alive!"

* * * * * * * *

"Well, aren't you going to call them again on the radio?" Sil asked Lance as they flew toward Redmond.

"No," said Lance. "We're out of simplex range by now, and besides, they've got better things to do than talk to me."

"You always keep those batteries charged, don't you?"

"Sure do," Lance said.

"Good idea."

Commander Bernaldi arrived at camp one minute before Marc and Kim. He was one of the first to greet them and help them out of the truck. After seeing that they were both okay, although disheveled and dirty, he left to return to communicate with the fire units still battling the blaze.

Someone handed Kim and Marc cups of water. Kim took hers and went around to the back of the truck. Cautiously, she opened the canopy. Brutus was lying on his side, his head barely raised, panting.

"Brutus?"

At her voice, he sat up.

"Here," she said, crawling into the pickup bed with him. She held the cup of water to his mouth and watched as he lapped it up greedily. "Could someone bring me a wet towel?" she asked.

A soaking wet rag was handed through to her. Kim took it and gently wiped the dog's hot body down. He looked at her and then settled back down on the truck bed. Another man had brought a bigger container of water, and she placed this next to Brutus before crawling back out. Gratefully, she drank the second cup of water she had been given. Someone else gave them cups of strong tea laced with honey. Surprisingly, the hot beverage tasted good, and Kim felt her energy begin to revive.

Kim's fire lookout supervisor, Don Kienzle, arrived from the Ranger Station. He took one glance at Kim's bedraggled condition and enveloped her in a big hug.

"Are you sure you're okay?" he said, holding her back, so he could observe the many bleeding scratches and burns on her exposed skin.

"Yes," she said, turning to Marc who had come to stand beside her. "I think we're both just fine."

* * * * * * * *

They stayed in the park for another hour. Both Kim and Marc called home from the Ranger Station to assure their parents that they were indeed alive and would be coming home soon.

None of their burns appeared to be serious. One of the paramedics put salve on a small second degree burn on Kim's leg and bandaged it. Kim laughed when she saw Marc hovering close to the back of his truck. The paint on the truck was badly blistered and scraped, but Marc seemed more concerned with what was in the truck.

"I know, I bet you want to see how your bass fared," she guessed correctly.

"Right, but there's someone in there beside it, and I'm not sure how he likes me."

"Here, Brutus." Kim snapped her fingers and the dog jumped down to her on the ground. Warily, watching the dog, Marc climbed in the truck.

"It's fine," he said smiling. "Not even a blister on the wood. This case must be better than I thought."

Kim sat on the ground, rubbing Brutus gently behind his ears, being careful not to touch the raw spots on his neck.

"How do you know his name is Brutus?" a young woman fire fighter asked Kim.

"Because that's what the men called him ... oh! I've just been so happy to be alive, I haven't even thought about them. Did they make it out alive?"

"One of them did."

Kim didn't ask any more questions. Instead, she turned her attention back to Brutus and briefly told Cheryl Meredith, the fire fighter, how the dog had saved their lives.

"He's a Pit Bull, you know," she said to Cheryl. "Yeah, I know," she laughed softly. "Haven't you noticed how the others are keeping their distance?"

Kim looked over at the other people milling around. Indeed, many of them did seem to have a cautious eye on Brutus at all times.

"But you're not afraid of him, are you?" Kim asked.

"No, I had a dog that looked just like him when I was a kid. Great dog—best friend I ever had."

"I'm afraid ol' Brutus here isn't everyone's friend. The men left him to guard me—I think they thought he would kill me. But we made a deal," Kim laughed, patting the dog.

"I saw what he did to one of them, though," she said somberly. "I'm not sure a dog who's been trained like this can ever be anyone's pet. I know I can't take him. We have a dog, and besides, I'm at college most of the year."

"Let me take him," Cheryl Meredith said. "He may have to be held as evidence by the sheriff's department until they decide what to do with the guy who got out, but when that's all settled, I'd like to give Brutus here a home."

She held out her hand to Brutus and to Kim's surprise, the dog sniffed it and allowed Cheryl to pet him.

"I live alone and I could keep him well fenced in. If it doesn't work, I'll have him put to sleep humanely, but I'd at least like to give him a chance. I live just down the road here about a quarter of a mile."

Kim watched as Cheryl walked over to talk to her supervisor. She came back with a rope and looped it gently around Brutus's neck. The dog followed her willingly as Cheryl led him toward his new home.

"Good luck, Brutus," Kim said softly.

* * * * * * * *

"Let's go home," Kim whispered to Marc. "My supervisor suggested it."

"Best idea I've heard all day," said Marc.

Chapter 24

Endings and Beginnings

Friday, September 2nd, 9 a.m.

"Y ou sure you don't want to ride?" Jack asked Kim as he led the mules up the Vista Peak trail ahead of her.

"Thanks, but no. I want to see everything close up—oh look, there's a clump of grass that's not burned," Kim said, kneeling down to examine it closer.

"Fire's funny that way," Jack said. "Takes one thing and skips over the next. But this one didn't do much skipping," he said, shaking his head sadly at the burned vista all around them.

The fire had been out for two days now, but smoke seeped up from the ground, and every breath of wind brought showers of ash from the charred trees still standing.

"The lookout's okay—you're sure?" Kim asked.

"Damaged on one end but definitely liveable," Jack assured her, "and I think your stuff inside is all okay too. In fact, even the outhouse survived."

Kim had wanted to go back up last Tuesday when Highway 22 reopened to local traffic, but her supervisor and her parents had insisted she take some time off.

"What is there to watch anyway?" her father questioned. "Isn't everything already burned?"

"In one direction, yes, but certainly not in the others," Kim told him.

The Staffords looked at their daughter curiously. Almost killed in a fire, and all she could think about was getting back to the lookout.

Now on the trail, Kim talked to Jack.

"This is just so sad," she said, turning over a dead chipmunk with a stick. "So much life was here, and now it's gone."

Jack looked back at her.

"It's hard when you see the effects of a fire, and all of us who work here in the forest feel like we've lost a family member when there's a big fire like this. But like it or not, Kim, fire is part of the natural cycle of the forest.

"This one wasn't—it was man-made—I've heard it was caused by someone camping, but there are many other devastating fires every year started by lightning. Next winter, the logging companies will be in here replanting trees, and Mother Nature will do some regeneration herself. It's all part of the life and death circle of the earth."

Kim smiled at Jack. It was the longest speech she'd ever heard him make. His words made her feel better. She looked out over the blackened valley and tried to imagine the ground bursting forth with new growth.

They rounded the last bend in the trail. Kim ran to the lookout. It was still standing—the house part of the structure was virtually untouched. One end of the catwalk had been singed, but the supports underneath seemed sound. She realized the fire earlier in the summer had burned the grass up close to the lookout, creating a firebreak that had channeled the fire around the lookout.

With tears of happiness in her eyes, Kim opened the door and went inside. The strong smell of smoke made her cough, but all her possessions, including "Jessie" were just as she'd left them.

"Whew," said Jack, propping the door open. "It's going to take a while to get that smoke out of here. You sure you want to stay?"

"Yes, I'm sure," Kim told him. "If I have to, I'll sleep outside."

"Well, tell you what. I'm not busy this morning. Let me help you get this place aired out."

Jack immediately began carrying her bedding out to hang over the rails. Everything that could be removed was taken outside, and he filled a bucket with bleach and water.

"You go ahead and do your watches, and I'll just scrub," he told Kim.

In between her quarter-hour scans, she helped him, and by noon, the interior of the lookout was smelling considerably fresher. Kim fixed Jack lunch and they talked on the deck for awhile before he left.

"Probably two more weeks, tops," he told her, "and the fire season will be over. There's supposed to be a rainstorm moving in next week."

"I have to go back to school on the 20th, anyway," Kim said. "It's going to seem strange being around so many people after the solitude of this lookout."

"That peacefulness is locked away in your mind, Kim—it's there to go to whenever you need to."

Kim smiled at Jack. What an amazing man he was.

"I'll remember that," she said, softly. "Thank you."

"And how's that young man of yours?" Jack asked, changing the subject.

"Fine," Kim said. "He's at home in Portland, but I think he's going to hike up here tomorrow to see me."

"There you go blushing again," Jack laughed. "He must be very special."

"You can't get much more special than risking your life for someone else," Kim said.

"Well then, get busy *woman*," Jack said, lightening the mood. "Bake him a pie, sweep the floor, tie a ribbon in your hair!"

"Okay, I'll do all of that," Kim agreed laughing.

They hugged good-bye, and Kim watched him disappear down the trail. She picked up the binoculars and studied the landscape carefully. Yes, it was black for several miles to the south of her, but the green backdrop of trees to the north and west was just as alive as before. Kim turned her body slowly, taking in every detail of the forests below. Suddenly, she saw a wisp of white smoke due north.

She ran inside to get an azimuth.

"Willamette Dispatch from Vista Peak, I have a smoke."

She rattled off the coordinates, surprised that she was the first to call them in.

"Copy, Vista Peak. And Kim ... welcome home."

Author's Note

Writing *Firewatch!* brought me back again to the beautiful Oregon Cascades, the setting for *Night Signals.*

Dangerous fires have threatened our beautiful woodlands in recent years due to very dry summers. But thanks to the watchfulness of the fire lookouts who guard our forests and the courage of the men and women who battle the fires, most of our forests are still intact. All of these tireless workers are to be commended for preserving our national resources.

Amateur Radio continues to be my favorite hobby. I hope this book will introduce you as readers to the fun of communication by radio. If you are interested in becoming an Amateur Radio operator, contact your local club or write the American Radio Relay League, 225 Main St., Newington, CT 06111 for more information.

This book would not have been possible without the technical advice and support of the following people. A sincere thank you to each of them, and a special thank you of remembrance to Captain Leon Riggs who passed away in December 1991.

Ann Anumdson, Coffin Mt. Lookout, U.S. Forest Service

Brian Ballou, Public Affairs Specialist, Oregon Dept. of Forestry

Michael Dietrich, Fuels Management Specialist, Bureau of Land Management

Stephanie Hazen, D.V.M., (former lookout)

Debi Klecker, Detective, Marion County Sheriff's Department

Ray Kresek, WA7YFM, Author of *Fire Lookouts of Oregon & Washington*

Lenore Jensen, W6NAZ

Steve Jensen, W6RHM

Brian Lash, Pilot Tanker 66, Redmond Air Center

Hollie Molesworth, KA7SJP

Captain Leon Riggs (ret), Marion County Sheriff's Department

Bonnie Walbran, Humane Society of the Willamette Valley

Bob Wall

Dave Wall

Michael Wall, KA7ITR

Bob Webb, Copilot Tanker 67, Redmond Air Center

Hope to hear you on the air!

Best Wishes,

Cynthia Wall, KA7ITT

Cynthia Wall, KA7ITT